The Adventures of Ulysses

Bernard Evslin

••••

With
Connected Readings

PRENTICE HALL
Upper Saddle River, New Jersey
Needham, Massachusetts

ISBN 0-13-437489-4

6 7 8 9 10   04

PRENTICE HALL

Acknowledgments

Grateful acknowledgment is made to the following for permission to reprint copyrighted material:

Ballantine Books, a division of Random House, Inc.
"The Reluctant Jedi" from *Star Wars: From the Adventures of Luke Skywalker* by George Lucas. Copyright © 1976 by The Star Wars Corporation. Reprinted by permission of Ballantine Books, a division of Random House, Inc.

Crown Publishers, Inc.
"The Wooden Horse" from *Classic Myths to Read Aloud* by William Russell. Copyright © 1989 by William F. Russell. Reprinted by permission of Crown Publishers, Inc.

Dutton Children's Books, a division of Penguin Putnam Inc., and David Higham
"Death of a Maiden" from *The Light Beyond the Forest* by Rosemary Sutcliff. Copyright © 1979 by Rosemary Sutcliff. Used by permission of Dutton Children's Books, a division of Penguin Putnam Inc., and David Higham Associates.

Enslow Publishers, Inc.
"Jacob Parrot: The First Medal of Honor Recipient" from *Congressional Medal of Honor Recipients* by Kieran Doherty. Copyright © 1998 by Kieran Doherty. Reprinted by permission of Enslow Publishers, Inc.

Houghton Mifflin Company and HarperCollins Publishers Ltd.
"Riddles in the Dark" and "Roads Go Ever Ever On" from *The Hobbitt* by J. R. R. Tolkien. Copyright © 1966 by J. R. R. Tolkien. All rights reserved. Reprinted by permission.

Lucasfilm, Ltd.
From *Raiders of the Lost Ark*, The Storybook Based on the Movie by Les Martin, based on a film, story by George Lucas and Philip Kaufman. Copyright © 1981 by Lucasfilm, Ltd.

(Acknowledgments continue on p. 172.)

Contents

The Adventures of Ulysses

Biographical Note

Homer Perhaps the most famous and widely read Greek poet of any age, Homer is believed to have composed his epic poems, the *Iliad* and the *Odyssey*, between 800 and 700 B.C. These poems tell the story of the Trojan War (an event that may have occurred in the mid-1200's B.C.) and the events that followed, as "seen" through the imagination of the blind poet. *The Adventures of Ulysses* by Bernard Evslin is a modern retelling of Homer's second poem, the *Odyssey*, which is the story of the long voyage of Odysseus—another name for Ulysses.

Names and Places in *The Adventures of Ulysses*

The Adventures of Ulysses is the tale of Ulysses on his ten-year journey home from the Trojan War. The following list identifies the important places, people, gods, and monsters that are part of Ulysses' adventures.

Ulysses' Crew

Elpenor (el´ pen ôr): Died on the journey to the Underworld, and became a ghost who advised Ulysses.

Eurylochus (yo͞o ril´ ə kəs): One of Ulysses' two underchiefs.

Perimedes (per´ ə mē´ dēz): One of Ulysses' two underchiefs.

Ulysses (yo͞o lis´ ēz´): King of Ithaca.

Places on Ulysses' Journey

Aegean (ē jē´ ən) Sea: Sea located between Turkey and Greece.

Ithaca (ith´ ə kə): Ulysses' home.

Libya (lib´ ē ə): Land of the Lotus-Eaters. The lotus caused sleep and pleasant dreams in those who ate the plant.

Ogygia (o jij´ ē ə): Home of Calypso.

Phaeacia (fē ā´ shä): Land where Ulysses washed up after his ship was destroyed in a storm.

Tartarus (tär´ tə rəs): The Underworld.

Thrinacia (thri nā´ shä): Island where the Sun-Titan (the Titans were predecessors to the Gods) kept his sacred cattle, later known as Sicily.

Gods and Goddesses

Aeolus (ē´ ə lis´): Son of Poseidon and keeper of the winds.

Amphitrite (am´ fi trīt´ ē): Poseidon's wife.

Apollo (ə päl´ ō): God of the sun.

Ares (er´ ēz´): God of war.

Artemis (är´ tə mis): Goddess of the hunt.

Athene (ə thē´ nē): Goddess of wisdom.

Demeter (di mēt´ ər): Goddess of the harvest.

Hades (hā´ dēz´): God of the Underworld.

Hermes (hur´ mēz´): Messenger of the gods.

Hypnos (hip´ näs´): God of sleep.

Morpheus (môr´ fē əs): God of dreams.

Persephone (pər səf´ ə nē): Daughter of Demeter and wife to Hades. It is her yearly descent into the Underworld that causes winter; her return brings spring.

Poseidon (pō sī´ dən): God of the sea and earthquakes. It is his hatred of Ulysses that causes the hardships and the long voyage.

Zeus (zo͞os): King of the gods.

Monsters and Other Enemies

Charybdis (ka rib´ dis): A monster who drinks so much water that she causes a whirlpool.

Circe (sʉr´ sē): Sorceress who captures Ulysses and turns his crew into pigs.

Polyphemus (päl´ i fē´ məs): A son of Poseidon and one of the Cyclopes (sī klō´ pēz), huge creatures with one gigantic eye in the middle of their foreheads.

Scylla (sil´ ə): A monster with twelve legs and six heads. She eats six sailors from any boat that sails too near her home.

Sirens (sī´ rənz): Sisters whose singing is so sweet that men will jump overboard to their deaths just to be closer to the singing.

Ghosts

Achilles (ə kil´ ēz´): The greatest warrior of the Trojan War. He was killed by a poison arrow that pierced his heel.

Ajax (ā´ jaks´): Another great warrior from the Trojan War.

Anticleia (an´ ti klē´ ə): Ulysses' mother.

Teiresias (tī rē´ sē əs): The sage whose advice Ulysses sought.

Others

Agelaus (ag´ ə lā´ əs): One of Penelope's suitors.

Alcinous (al sin´ ō əs): King of Phaeacia.

Antinous (an tin´ ō əs): One of Penelope's suitors.

Arete (ä rē´ tē): Queen of Phaeacia.

Calypso (kə lip´ sō): One of the Titans who keeps Ulysses prisoner on her island.

Ciconians (ki kō´ nē uns): A group of villagers and hillmen that Ulysses and his crew tried to raid. Ulysses' failure here was the beginning of his long years of bad luck.

Eumaeus (ū mē´ us): The person in charge of Ulysses' herd of swine (pigs).

Euryalus (yo͞o rē´ ə ləs): A warrior of Phaeacia.

Eurycleia (yo͞o´ ri klē´ ə): Ulysses' nurse when he was a boy.

Eurymachus (yo͞o ri´ mə kəs): The leader of Penelope's suitors.

Ino (ēn´ ō): A Nereid (nir´ ē id), or minor sea goddess, who saves Ulysses from drowning.

Iros (ī´ rəs): A beggar in Ulysses' home.

Nausicaa (no sik´ ä ä): Princess of Phaeacia.

Penelope (pə nel´ ə pē): Ulysses' wife.

Telemachus (tə lem´ ə kəs): Ulysses' son.

Prologue

THE adventures of Ulysses begin many years before the opening of this book. He was the master strategist of the Greek forces in their war against Troy, the war that started with an apple, ended with a horse, and was fought by a thousand kings for the love of a single woman. It left an ancient city in flames that still burn in man's imagination after three thousand years.

The war started when Peleus, mightiest hero of his time, was married to Thetis, the most beautiful naiad that ever sported among the waves or fled the embrace of Poseidon. It was a magnificent wedding, attended by all the gods on Olympus. Unfortunately, however, Thetis had neglected to send an invitation to Eris, Lady of Discord and sister to the God of War. It was an omission that was to cost a river of blood. For Eris came without invitation and threw upon the banquet table a golden apple inscribed "To The Fairest." Mischievous words! The apple was claimed immediately by Hera (Queen of the Gods), Athene (Goddess of Wisdom), and Aphrodite (Goddess of Love).

The feud between the three goddesses waxed so bitter that no god dared attempt mediation but passed judgment on to Paris, a shepherd boy of Troy, the son of King Priam, whose royal birth had been kept secret. Paris was said to be the most beautiful of all the lads of the Inner Sea.

Bribes came his way immediately. Hera offered him power, promising to make him the mightiest king the world had ever seen. Athene offered him wisdom. All the lore of heaven and earth, and all the lore beyond death, too—all that has been written and spoken, and also that too secret to be uttered, would be his. Aphrodite said little. She came close to him and whispered in his ear. When she had finished whispering, he gave her the apple. She smiled and kissed him. Hera and Athene flew off, screaming their rage.

What the Goddess Aphrodite had whispered to Paris was a promise—that he should have any woman he looked upon with desire. She then recommended the most desirable, a Spartan queen named Helen, who the goddess said was the mortal most resembling herself. In fact, Helen was by way of being a relative, for she had been born of Leda, who had been loved by Zeus disguised as a swan, and so she herself had the radiant stature of the gods, a swan's soft muscularity, and her mother's eyes. Paris straightaway gave up being a shepherd and resumed his rank as Prince of Troy. He demanded of his doting father a treasure ship and a piratical crew. Thereupon he sailed to Sparta on a diplomatic mission to King Menelaus, Helen's husband. Paris and Helen met at a state banquet. By dawn she was aboard his ship and it was sailing for Troy.

Now, Helen had been courted by all the kings and princes of the Greek islands. Her father had hesitated long before allowing her to accept any suitor. He was afraid that the rejected suitors would band together to destroy the successful one—and himself and his kingdom in the bargain. So Helen flirted with them all, encouraged them all, and accepted none. Finally, Ulysses, who was one of the suitors, offered a plan. All Helen's admirers would swear a mighty oath to refrain from murdering the successful suitor and would join to defend Helen and her husband—whoever he might be—against any attack.

Thereupon Helen chose Menelaus, King of Sparta, most powerful of the Greek chieftains. Thus it was that when Paris made off with Helen, a thousand kings were summoned to keep their oath. They assembled a huge fleet and sailed for Troy.

The Greeks camped outside the walls of Troy, and for ten years tried to fight their way into the city. But the walls were strong and the Trojans brave. The defenders were led by King Priam's fifty warrior sons. The great Hector was their chief. And even after Hector was killed by the Greek hero, Achilles, the Trojans refused to be defeated—until they were tricked into defeating themselves.

The author of that fatal trick was Ulysses, sharpest tactician among the invaders. The Greeks pretended to lift their siege. They struck their tents, boarded their ships, and sailed around a headland out of sight, where they anchored and waited until nightfall. Behind them on the beach they had left a giant wooden horse. The Trojans reacted just as Ulysses had calculated. They began to celebrate and quickly lost their wits. They thought the wooden horse an offering to Poseidon, God of the Sea, and dragged it through the gates into the city, so as to anger Poseidon against the Greeks and spoil the voyage home. But the wooden horse was hollow, and so artfully made that Ulysses and a company of armed warriors were able to hide inside and remain undetected as the horse was rolled into the city. That night, as Troy slept, the Greeks crawled out of their hiding place, killed the Trojan sentries, and opened the gates to the Greek army, which had sailed back in the darkness.

It was a complete surprise. Troy was taken, its fighting men slaughtered, its women and children enslaved. Then Ulysses sailed for home, his three ships loaded with booty. But victory never comes cheap. Poseidon's anger had indeed been kindled. He roused the winds and tides against Ulysses and sent word to island ogres and monsters of the deep.

And for ten long years the great voyager had to battle his way through the worst perils that the imagination of an offended god could devise.

This is the story of that voyage.

Ships and Men

AFTER Troy was burned, Ulysses sailed for home with three ships holding fifty men each.

Three thousand years ago ships were very different; through the years they have changed much more than the men who sail them.

These beaked warships used by the pirate kingdoms of the Middle Sea were like no vessels you have ever seen. Imagine a very long narrow rowboat with twenty oars on each side. The timbers of the bow curve sharply to a prow, and this prow grows longer and sharper, becomes in fact a long, polished shaft tipped by a knife-edged brass spearhead. This was called the ram, the chief weapon of ancient warships.

In battle, the opposing ships spun about each other, swooping forward, twirling on their beams, darting backward, their narrow hulls allowing them to backwater very swiftly. The object was to ram the enemy before he rammed you. And to ram first was the only defense, for the brass beak of the ramming ship sheared easily through the timbers of its victim, knocking a huge hole in the hull and sinking it before its men could jump overboard.

These warships were also equipped with sail and mast—used only for voyaging, never in battle—a square sail, and a short mast, held fast by oxhide stays. The sail was raised only for a fair wind, or could be tilted slightly for a quartering wind, but was useless against headwinds.

This meant that these ships were almost always at the mercy of the weather and were often blown off course. Another thing that made them unfit for long voyages was the lack of cargo space. Only a few days' supply of food and water could be carried, leaving space for no other cargo. That is why these fighting ships tried to hug the coast and avoid the open sea.

Ulysses' problem was made worse by victory. When Troy was sacked, he and his men captured a huge booty—gold and jewels, silks, furs—and after ten years of war, the men refused to leave any loot behind. This meant that each of his ships could carry food and water for a very few days.

This greed for treasure caused many of his troubles at first. But then troubles came so thick and fast that no one could tell what caused them; hardships were simply called bad luck, or the anger of the gods.

But bad luck makes good stories.

The Ciconians

THE voyage began peacefully. A fair northeast wind blew, filling the sails of the little fleet and pushing it steadily homeward. The wind freshened at night, and the three ships scudded along joyfully under a fat moon.

On the morning of the second day Ulysses saw a blue haze of smoke and a glint of white stone. He put in toward shore and saw a beautiful little town. The men stared in amazement at this city without walls, rich with green parks and grazing cattle, its people strolling about in white tunics. Ten years of war had made Ulysses' men as savage as wolves. Everyone not a shipmate was an enemy. To meet was to fight; property belonged to the winner.

Ulysses stood in the bow, shading his eyes with his hand, gazing at the city. A tough, crafty old warrior named Eurylochus stood beside him.

"We attack, do we not?" he asked. "The city lies there defenseless. We can take it without losing a man."

"Yes, it looks tempting," said Ulysses. "But the wind blows fair, and good fortune attends us. Perhaps it will spoil our luck to stop."

"But this fat little city has been thrown into our laps by the gods, too," said Eurylochus, "and they grow angry when men refuse their gifts. It would be bad luck *not* to attack."

Ulysses heard the fierce murmur of his men behind him and felt their greed burning in his veins. He hailed the other ships and gave orders, and the three black-hulled vessels swerved toward shore and nosed into the harbor, swooping down upon the white city like wolves upon a sheepfold.

They landed on the beach. The townsfolk fled before them into the hills. Ulysses did not allow his men to pursue them, for there was no room on the ship for slaves. From house to house the armed men went, helping themselves to whatever they wanted. Afterward they piled the booty in great heaps upon the beach.

Then Ulysses had them round up a herd of the plump, swaying, crook-horned cattle, and offer ten bulls in sacrifice to the gods. Later they built huge bonfires on the beach, roasted the cattle, and had a great feast.

But while the looting and feasting was going on, the men of the city had withdrawn into the hills and called together their kinsmen of the villages, the Ciconians, and began preparing for battle. They were skillful fighters, these men of the hills. They drove brass war chariots that had long blades attached to the wheels, and these blades whirled swiftly as the wheels turned, scything down the foe.

They gathered by the thousands, an overwhelming force, and stormed down out of the hills onto the beach. Ulysses' men were full of food and wine, unready to fight, but he had posted sentries, who raised a shout when they saw the Ciconians coming down from the hills in the moonlight. Ulysses raged among his men, slapping them with the flat of his sword, driving the fumes of wine out of their heads. His great racketing battle cry roused those he could not whip with his sword.

The men closed ranks and met the Ciconians at spearpoint. The Hellenes retreated slowly, leaving their treasure where it was heaped upon the beach and, keeping their line unbroken, made for their ships.

Ulysses chose two of his strongest men and bade them lift a thick timber upon their shoulders. He sat astride this timber, high enough to shoot his arrows over the heads of his men. He was the most skillful archer since Heracles. He aimed only at the chariot horses, and aimed not to kill, but to cripple, so that the horses fell in their traces, and their furious flailing and kicking broke the enemy's advance.

Thus the Hellenes were able to reach their ships, roll them into the water, leap into the rowers' benches, and row away. But eighteen men were left dead on the beach—six from each ship— and there was scarcely a man unwounded.

Eurylochus threw himself on his knees before Ulysses and said: "I advised you badly, O Chief. We have angered the gods. Perhaps, if you kill me, they will be appeased."

"Eighteen dead are enough for one night." said Ulysses. "Our luck has changed, but what has changed can change again. Rise and go about your duties."

The ships had been handled roughly in the swift retreat from the Ciconian beach. Their hulls had been battered by axes and flung spears, and they had sprung small leaks. The wind had faded to a whisper, and the men were forced to row with water sloshing around their ankles. Ulysses saw that his ships were foundering and that he would have to empty the holds. Food could not be spared, nor water; the only thing that could go was the treasure taken from Troy. The men groaned and tore at their beards as they saw the gold and jewels and bales of fur and silk being dropped overboard. But Ulysses cast over his own share of the treasure first—and his was the largest share— so the men had to bite back their rage and keep on rowing.

As the necklaces, bracelets, rings, and brooches sank slowly, winking their jewels like drowned fires, a strange thing happened. A shoal of naiads—beautiful water nymphs—were drawn by the flash of the jewels. They dived after the bright baubles and swam alongside the ships, calling to the men, singing, tweaking the oars out of their hands, for they were sleek, mischievous creatures who loved jewels and strangers. Some of them came riding dolphins, and in the splashing silver veils of spray the men thought they saw beautiful girls with fishtails. This is probably how the first report of mermaids arose.

Poseidon, God of the Sea, was wakened from sleep by the sound of this laughter. When he saw what was happening, his green beard bristled with rage, and he said to himself:

"Can it be? Are these the warriors whom I helped in their siege of Troy? Is this their gratitude, trying to steal my naiads from me? I'll teach them manners."

He whistled across the horizon to his son, Aeolus, keeper of the winds, who twirled his staff and sent a northeast gale skipping across the sea. It pounced upon the little fleet and scattered the ships like twigs. Ulysses clung to the helm, trying to hold the kicking tiller, trying to shout over the wind. There was nothing to do but ship the mast and let the wind take them.

And the wind, in one huge gust of fury, drove them around Cythera, the southernmost of their home islands, into the open waters of the southwest quarter of the Middle Sea, toward the hump of Africa called Libya.

The Lotus-Eaters

NOW, at this time, the shore of Libya was known as "The land where Morpheus plays."

Who was Morpheus? He was a young god, son of Hypnos, God

of Sleep, and nephew of Hades. It was his task to fly around the world, from nightfall to dawn, scattering sleep. His father, Hypnos, mixed the colors of sleep for him, making them dark and thick and sad.

"For," he said, "it is a little death you lay upon man each night, my son, to prepare him for the kingdom of death."

But his aunt, Persephone, sewed him a secret pocket, full of bright things, and said:

"It is not death you scatter, but repose. Hang the walls of sleep with bright pictures, so that man may not know death before he dies."

These bright pictures were called dreams. And Morpheus became fascinated by the way a little corner of man's mind remained awake in sleep, and played with the colors he had hung, mixing them, pulling them apart, making new pictures. It seemed to him that these fantastic colored shadows the sleepers painted were the most beautiful, most puzzling things he had ever seen. And he wanted to know more about how they came to be.

He went to Persephone and said, "I need a flower that makes sleep. It must be purple and black. But there should be one petal streaked with fire-red, the petal to make dreams."

Persephone smiled and moved her long white hand in the air. Between her fingers a flower blossomed. She gave it to him.

"Here it is, Morpheus. Black and purple like sleep, with one petal of fire-red for dreams. We will call it lotus."

Morpheus took the flower and planted it in Libya, where it is always summer. The flower grew in clusters, smelling deliciously of honey. The people ate nothing else. They slept all the time, except when they were gathering flowers. Morpheus watched over them, reading their dreams.

It was toward Lotusland that Ulysses and his men were blown by the gale. The wind fell while they were still offshore. The sky cleared, the sea calmed, a hot sun beat down. To Ulysses, dizzy with fatigue, weak with hunger, the sky and the water and the air between seemed to flow together in one hot blueness.

He shook his head, trying to shake away the hot blue haze, and growled to his men to unship the oars and row toward land. The exhausted men bent to the oars, and the ships crawled over the fire-blue water. With their last strength they pulled the ships up on the beach, past the high-tide mark, and then lay down and went to sleep.

As they slept, the Lotus-eaters came out of the forest. Their arms were heaped with flowers, which they piled about the sleeping men in great blue and purple bouquets, so that they might have flowers to eat when they awoke, for these people were very gentle and hospitable.

The men awoke and smelled the warm, honey smell of the flowers and ate them in great handfuls—like honeycomb—and fell asleep again. Morpheus hovered over the sleeping men and read their dreams.

"These men have done terrible things," the god whispered to himself. "Their dreams are full of gold and blood and fire. Such sleep will not rest them."

And he mixed them some cool green and silver dreams of home. The nightmares faded. Wounded Trojans stopped screaming, Troy stopped burning; they saw their wives smile, heard their children laugh, saw the green wheat growing in their own fields. They dreamed of home, awoke and were hungry, ate the honeyed lotus flowers, and fell into a deeper sleep.

Then Morpheus came to Ulysses, who was stretched on the sand, a little apart from the rest. He studied his face—the wide, grooved brow, the sunken eyes, the red hair, the jutting chin. And he said to himself: "This man is a hero. Terrible are his needs, sudden his deeds, and his dreams must be his own. I cannot help him."

So Morpheus mixed no colors for Ulysses' sleep but let him dream his own dreams and read them as they came. He hovered above the sleeping king and could not leave.

"What monsters he makes," he said to himself. "Look at that giant with the single eye in the middle of his forehead. And that terrible spiderwoman with all those legs . . . Ah, the things he dreams, this angry sleeper. What bloody mouths, what masts falling, sails ripping, what rocks and reefs, what shipwrecks . . . How many deaths?"

Ulysses awoke, choking, out of a terrible nightmare. It seemed to him that in his sleep he had seen the whole voyage laid out before him, had seen his ships sinking, his men drowning. Monsters had crowded about him, clutching, writhing. He sat up and looked about. His men lay asleep among heaped flowers. As he watched, one opened his eyes, raised himself on an elbow, took a handful of flowers, stuffed them into his mouth, and immediately fell asleep again.

Ulysses smelled the honey sweetness and felt an overpowering hunger. He took some of the flowers and raised them to his mouth. As their fragrance grew stronger, he felt his eyelids drooping, his arms growing heavy, and he thought: "It is these flowers that are making us sleep. Their scent alone brings sleep. I must not eat them."

But he could not put them down; his hand would not obey him. Exerting all the bleak force of his will, he grasped his right hand with his left—as if it belonged to someone else—and one by one forced open his fingers and let the flowers fall.

Then he dragged himself to his feet and walked slowly into the sea. He went under and arose snorting. His head had cleared. But when he went up on the beach, the sweet fragrance rose like an ether and made him dizzy again.

"I must work swiftly," he said.

One by one he carried the sleeping men to the ships and propped them on their benches. His strength was going. The honey smell was invading him, making him droop with sleep. He took his knife and, cutting sharp splinters of wood to prop open his eyelids, staggered back among the men. He worked furiously now, lifting them on his shoulders, carrying them two at a time, throwing them into the ships.

Finally, the beach was cleared. The men lolled sleeping upon the benches. Then, all by himself, using his last strength, he pushed the ships into the water. When the ships were afloat in the shallow water, he lashed one to another with rawhide line, his own ship in front. Then he raised his sail and took the helm.

The wind was blowing from the southwest. It filled his sail. The line grew taut; the file of ships moved away from Lotusland.

The men began to awake from their dreams of home and found themselves upon the empty sea again. But the long sleep had rested them, and they took up their tasks with new strength.

Ulysses kept the helm, grim and unsmiling. For he knew that what he had seen painted on the walls of his sleep was meant to come true and that he was sailing straight into a nightmare.

The Cyclops' Cave

AFTER he had rescued his crew from Lotusland, Ulysses found that he was running from one trouble into another. They were still at sea, and there was no food for the fleet. The men were hungry and getting dangerous. Ulysses heard them grumbling: "He should have left us there in Lotusland. At least when you're asleep you don't know you're hungry. Why did he have to come and wake us up?" He knew that unless he found food for them very soon he would be facing a mutiny.

That part of the Aegean Sea was dotted with islands. On every one of them was a different kind of enemy. The last thing Ulysses wanted to do was to go ashore, but there was no other way of getting food. He made a landfall on a small, mountainous island. He was very careful; he had the ships of the fleet moor offshore and selected twelve of his bravest men as a landing party.

They beached their skiff and struck inland. It was a wild, hilly place, full of boulders, with very few trees. It seemed deserted. Then Ulysses glimpsed something moving across the valley, on the slope of a hill. He was too far off to see what they were, but he thought they must be goats since the hill was so steep. And if they were goats they had to be caught. So the men headed downhill, meaning to cross the valley and climb the slope.

Ulysses had no way of knowing it, but in the entire sea this was the very worst island on which the small party could have landed. For here lived the Cyclopes, huge savage creatures, tall as trees, each with one eye in the middle of his forehead. Once, long ago, they had lived in the bowels of Olympus, forging thunderbolts for Zeus. But he had punished them for some fault, exiling them to this island where they had forgotten all their smithcraft and did nothing but fight with each other for the herds of wild goats, trying to find enough food to fill their huge bellies. Best of all, they liked storms; storms meant shipwrecks. Shipwrecks meant sailors struggling in the sea, who could be plucked out and eaten raw; and the thing they loved best in the world was human flesh. The largest and the fiercest and the hungriest of all the Cyclopes on the island was one named Polyphemus. He kept constant vigil on his mountain, in fair weather or foul. If he spotted a ship, and there was no storm to help, he would dive into the sea and swim underwater, coming up underneath the ship and overturning it. Then he would swim off with his pockets full of sailors.

On this day he could not believe his luck when he saw a boat actually landing on the beach and thirteen meaty-looking sailors disembark and begin to march toward his cave. But there they were, climbing out of the valley now, up the slope of the hill, right toward the cave. He realized they must be hunting his goats.

The door of the cave was an enormous slab of stone. He shoved this aside so that the cave stood invitingly open, casting a faint glow of firelight upon the dusk. Over the fire, on a great spit, eight goats were turning and roasting. The delicious savors of the cooking drifted from the cave. Polyphemus lay down behind a huge boulder and waited.

The men were halfway up the slope of the hill when they smelled the meat roasting. They broke into a run. Ulysses tried to restrain them, but they paid no heed—they were too hungry. They raced to the mouth of the cave and dashed in. Ulysses drew his sword and hurried after them. When he saw the huge fireplace and the eight goats spitted like sparrows, his heart sank because he knew that they had come into reach of something much larger than themselves. However, the men were giving no thought to anything but food; they flung themselves on the spit and tore into the goat meat, smearing their hands and faces with sizzling fat, too hungry to feel pain as they crammed the hot meat into their mouths.

There was a loud rumbling sound; the cave darkened. Ulysses whirled around. He saw that the door had been closed. The far end of the cavern was too dark to see anything, but then—amazed, aghast—he saw what looked like a huge red lantern far above, coming closer. Then he saw the great shadow of a nose under it and the gleam of teeth. He realized that the lantern was a great flaming eye. Then he saw the whole giant, tall as a tree, with huge fingers reaching out of the shadows, fingers bigger than baling hooks. They closed around two sailors and hauled them screaming into the air.

As Ulysses and his horrified men watched, the great hand bore the struggling little men to the giant's mouth. He ate them, still wriggling, the way a cat eats a grasshopper; he ate them clothes and all, growling over their raw bones.

The men had fallen to their knees and were whimpering like terrified children, but Ulysses stood there, sword in hand, his agile brain working more swiftly than it ever had before.

"Greetings," he called. "May I know to whom we are indebted for such hospitality?"

The giant belched and spat out buttons. "I am Polyphemus," he growled. "This is my cave, my mountain, and everything that comes here is mine. I do hope you can all stay to dinner. There are just enough of you to make a meal. Ho, ho . . ." And he laughed a great, choking, phlegmy laugh, swiftly lunged, and caught another sailor, whom he lifted into the air and held before his face.

"Wait!" cried Ulysses.

"What for?"

"You won't enjoy him that way. He is from Attica, where the olives grow. He was raised on olives and has a very delicate, oily flavor. But to appreciate it, you must taste the wine of the country."

"Wine? What is wine?"

"It is a drink. Made from pressed grapes. Have you never drunk it?"

"We drink nothing but ox blood and buttermilk here."

"Ah, you do not know what you have missed, gentle Polyphemus. Meat-eaters, in particular, love wine. Here, try it for yourself."

Ulysses unslung from his belt a full flask of unwatered wine. He gave it to the giant, who put it to his lips and gulped. He coughed violently and stuck the sailor in a little niche high up in the cave wall, then leaned his great slab of a face toward Ulysses and said:

"What did you say this drink was?"

"Wine. A gift of the gods to man, to make women look better and food taste better. And now it is my gift to you."

"It's good, very good." He put the flask to his lips and swallowed again. "You are very polite. What's your name?"

"My name? Why I am—nobody."

"Nobody . . . Well, Nobody, I like you. You're a good fellow. And do you know what I'm going to do? I'm going to save you till last. Yes, I'll eat all your friends first, and give you extra time, that's what I'm going to do."

Ulysses looked up into the great eye and saw that it was redder than ever. It was all a swimming redness. He had given the monster, who had never drunk spirits before, undiluted wine. Surely it must make him sleepy. But was a gallon enough for that great gullet? Enough to put him to sleep—or would he want to eat again first?

"Eat 'em all up, Nobody—save you till later. Sleep a little first. Shall I? Won't try to run away, will you? No—you can't, can't open the door—too heavy, ha, ha. . . . You take a nap, too, Nobody. I'll wake you for breakfast. Breakfast . . ."

The great body crashed full-length on the cave floor, making the very walls of the mountain shake. Polyphemus lay on his back, snoring like a powersaw. The sailors were still on the floor, almost dead from fear.

"Up!" cried Ulysses. "Stand up like men! Do what must be done! Or you will be devoured like chickens."

He got them to their feet and drew them about him as he explained his plan.

"Listen now, and listen well, for we have no time. I made him drunk, but we cannot tell how long it will last."

Ulysses thrust his sword into the fire; they saw it glow white-hot.

"There are ten of us," he said. "Two of us have been eaten, and one of our friends is still unconscious up there on his shelf of rock. You four get on one side of his head, and the rest on the other side. When I give the word, lay hold of the ear on your side, each of you. And hang on, no matter how he thrashes, for I am going to put out his eye. And if I am to be sure of my stroke, you must hold his head still. One stroke is all I will be allowed."

Then Ulysses rolled a boulder next to the giant's head and climbed on it, so that he was looking down into the eye. It was lidless and misted with sleep—big as a furnace door and glowing softly like a banked fire. Ulysses looked at his men. They had done what he said, broken into two parties, one group at each ear. He lifted his white-hot sword.

"Now!" he cried.

Driving down with both hands and all the strength of his back and shoulders and all his rage and all his fear, Ulysses stabbed the glowing spike into the giant's eye.

His sword jerked out of his hand as the head flailed upward; men pelted to the ground as they lost their hold. A huge screeching, curdling bellow split the air.

"This way!" shouted Ulysses.

He motioned to his men, and they crawled on their bellies toward the far end of the cave where the herd of goats was tethered. They slipped into the herd and lay among the goats as the giant stomped about the cave, slapping the walls with great blows of his hands, picking up boulders and cracking them together in agony, splitting them to cinders, clutching his eye, a scorched hole now, from which the brown blood jelled. He moaned and gibbered and bellowed in frightful pain; his groping hand found the sailor in the wall, and he tore him to pieces between his fingers. Ulysses could not even hear the man scream because the giant was bellowing so.

Now Ulysses saw that the Cyclops' wild stampeding was giving place to a plan. For now he was stamping on the floor in a regular pattern, trying to find and crush them beneath his feet. He stopped moaning and listened. The sudden silence dazed the men with fear. They held their breath and tried to muffle the sound of their beating hearts; all the giant heard was the breathing of the goats. Then Ulysses saw him go to the mouth of the cave and swing the great slab aside and stand there. He realized just in time that the goats would rush outside, which is what the giant wanted, for then he could search the whole cave.

Ulysses whispered: "Quickly, swing under the bellies of the rams. Hurry, hurry!"

17

Luckily, they were giant goats and thus able to carry the men who had swung themselves under their bellies and were clinging to the wiry wool. Ulysses himself chose the largest ram. They moved toward the mouth of the cave and crowded through. The Cyclops' hands came down and brushed across the goats' backs feeling for the men, but the animals were huddled too closely together for him to reach between and search under their bellies. So he let them pass through.

Now the Cyclops rushed to the corner where the goats had been tethered and stamped, searched, and roared through the whole cave again, bellowing with fury when he did not find them. The herd grazed on the slope of the hill beneath the cave. There was a full moon; it was almost bright as day.

"Stay where you are," Ulysses whispered.

He heard a crashing, peered out, and saw great shadowy figures converging on the cave. He knew that the other Cyclopes of the island must have heard the noise and had come to see. He heard the giant bellow.

The others called to him: "Who has done it? Who has blinded you?"

"Nobody. Nobody did it. Nobody blinded me."

"Ah, you have done it yourself. What a tragic accident."

And they went back to their own caves.

"Now!" said Ulysses. "Follow me!"

He swung himself out from under the belly of the ram and raced down the hill. The others raced after him. They were halfway across the valley when they heard great footsteps rushing after them, and Polyphemus bellowing nearer and nearer.

"He's coming!" cried Ulysses. "Run for your lives!"

They ran as they had never run before, but the giant could cover fifty yards at a stride. It was only because he could not see and kept bumping into trees and rocks that they were able to reach the skiff and push out on the silver water before Polyphemus burst out of the grove of trees and rushed onto the beach. They bent to the oars, and the boat scudded toward the fleet.

Polyphemus heard the dip of the oars and the groaning of the oarlocks and, aiming at the sound, hurled huge boulders after them. They fell all around the ship but did not hit. The skiff reached Ulysses' ship, and the sailors climbed aboard.

"Haul anchor, and away!" cried Ulysses. And then called to the Cyclops: "Poor fool! Poor blinded, drunken, gluttonous fool— if anyone else asks you, it is not Nobody, but Ulysses who has done this to you."

But he was to regret this final taunt. The gods honor courage but punish pride.

Polyphemus, wild with rage, waded out chest-deep and hurled a last boulder, which hit mid-deck, almost sunk the ship, and killed most of the crew—among them seven of the nine men who had just escaped.

And Polyphemus prayed to Poseidon: "God of the Sea, I beg you, punish Ulysses for this. Visit him with storm and shipwreck and sorceries. Let him wander many years before he reaches home, and when he gets there let him find himself forgotten, unwanted, a stranger."

Poseidon heard this prayer and made it all happen just that way.

Keeper of the Winds

NOW the black ships beat their way northward from the land of the Cyclopes. And Ulysses, ignorant of the mighty curse that the blind giant had fastened upon him, was beginning to hope that they might have fair sailing the rest of the way home. So impatient was he that he took the helm himself and kept it night and day although his sailors pleaded with him to take some rest. But he was wild with eagerness to get home to his wife Penelope, to his young son Telemachus, and to the dear land of Ithaca that he had not seen for more than ten years now.

At the end of the third night, just as the first light was staining the sky, he saw something very strange—a wall of bronze, tall and wide, floating on the sea and blocking their way. At first he thought it was a trick of the light, and he rubbed his eyes and looked again. But there it was, a towering, bright wall of beaten bronze.

"Well," he thought to himself, "it cannot stretch across the sea. There must be a way to get around it."

He began to sail along the wall as though it were the shore of an island, trying to find his way around. Finally, he came to a huge gate, and even as he gazed upon it in amazement, the gate swung open and the wind changed abruptly. The shrouds snapped, the sails bulged, the masts groaned, and all three ships of the fleet were blown through the gate, which immediately clanged shut behind them. Once within the wall, the wind fell off and Ulysses found his ship drifting toward a beautiful, hilly island. Suddenly there was a great howling of wind. The sun was blown out like a candle. Darkness fell upon the waters. Ulysses felt the deck leap beneath him as the ship was lifted halfway out of the water by the ferocious gust and hurled through the blackness. He tried to shout, but the breath was torn from his mouth, and he lost consciousness.

Ulysses had no way of knowing this, but the mischievous Poseidon had guided his ships to the island fortress of Aeolus, Keeper of the Winds. Ages before, when the world was very new, the gods had become fearful of the terrible strength of the winds and had decided to tame them. So Zeus and Poseidon, working together, had floated an island upon the sea and girdled it about with a mighty bronze wall. Then they set a mountain upon the island and hollowed out that mountain until it was a huge stone dungeon. Into this hollow mountain they stuffed the struggling winds and appointed Aeolus as their jailer. And there the winds were held captive. Whenever the gods wanted to stir up a storm and needed a particular wind, they sent a message to Aeolus, who would draw his sword and stab the side of the mountain, making a hole big enough for the wind to fly through. If the north wind were wanted, he stabbed the north side of the mountain, its east slope for the east wind, and so on. When the storm was done, he would whistle the wind home, and the huge brawling gale, broken by its imprisonment, would crawl back whimpering to its hole.

Aeolus was an enormously fat demigod with a long wind-tangled beard and a red and wind-beaten face. He loved to eat and drink, and fight, play games, and hear stories. Twelve children he had, six boys and six girls. He sent them out one by one, riding the back of the wind around the world, managing the weather for each month.

And it was in the great castle of Aeolus that Ulysses and his men found themselves when they awoke from their enchanted sleep. Invisible hands held torches for them, guided them to the baths, anointed them with oil, and gave them fresh clothing. Then the floating torches led them to the dining hall, where they were greeted by Aeolus and his twelve handsome children. A mighty banquet was laid before them, and they ate like starved men.

Then Aeolus said: "Strangers, you are my guests—uninvited—but guests all the same. By the look of you, you have had adventures and should have fine stories to tell. Yes, I love a tale full of fighting and blood and tricks, and if you have such to tell, then I shall entertain you royally. But if you are such men as sit dumb, glowering, unwilling to please, using your mouths only to stuff food into—then—well, then you are apt to find things less pleasant. You, Captain!" he roared, pointing at Ulysses. "You, sir—I take you for the leader of this somewhat motley crew. Do you have a story to tell?"

"For those who know how to listen, I have a tale to tell," said Ulysses.

"Your name?"

"Ulysses—of Ithaca."

"Mmm—yes," said Aeolus. "I seem to recognize that name— believe I heard it on Olympus while my uncles and aunts up there were quarreling about some little skirmish they had interested themselves in. Near Troy I think it was . . . Yes-s-s . . . Were you there?"

"I was there," said Ulysses. "I was there for ten years, dear host, and indeed took part in some of that petty skirmishing that will be spoken of by men who love courage when this bronze wall and this island, and you and yours, have vanished under the sea and have been forgotten for a thousand years. I am Ulysses. My companions before Troy were Achilles, Menelaus, Agamemnon, mighty heroes all, and, in modesty, I was not least among them."

"Yes-s-s . . ." said Aeolus. "You are bold enough. Too bold for your own good, perhaps. But you have caught my attention, Captain. I am listening. Tell on. . . ."

Then Ulysses told of the Trojan War; of the abduction of Helen, and the chase, and the great battles; the attacks, the retreats, the separate duels. He spoke of Achilles fighting Hector and killing him with a spear thrust, of Paris ambushing Achilles; and, finally, how he himself had made a great hollow wooden horse and had the Greek armies pretend to leave, only to sneak back and hide in the belly of the horse. He told how the Trojans had dragged the horse within their gates, and how the Greek warriors had crept out at night and taken the city and slaughtered their enemies.

Aeolus shouted with laughter. His face blazed and his belly shook. "Ah, that's a trick after my own heart!" he cried. "You're a sharp one, you are . . . I knew you had a foxy look about you. Wooden horse—ho ho! Tell more! Tell more!"

Then Ulysses told of his wanderings after the fall of Troy, of his adventure in Lotusland, and what had happened in the Cyclops' cave. And when Aeolus heard how he had outwitted Polyphemus and blinded his single eye, he struck the table with a mighty blow of his fist and shouted, "Marvelous! A master stroke! By the gods, you are the bravest, craftiest warrior that has ever drunk my wine." He was especially pleased because he had always hated Polyphemus. He had no way of knowing, of course, that the blinded Cyclops had prayed to his father and had laid a curse on Ulysses, and that he, Aeolus, was being made the instrument of that curse. He did not know this, for the gods move in mysterious ways. And so he roared with laughter and shouted, "You have pleased me, Ulysses. You have told me a brave tale, a tale full of blood and tricks. . . . And now I shall grant you any favor within my power. Speak out, Ulysses. Ask what you will."

"But one thing I seek, generous Aeolus," said Ulysses, "your help. I need your help in getting home. For it has been a long, weary time since we saw our homes and our families. Our hearts thirst for the sight of Ithaca."

"No one can help you better than I," said Aeolus. "You sail on ships, and I am Keeper of the Winds. Come with me."

He led Ulysses out into the night. A hot orange moon rode low in the sky, and they could see without torches. Aeolus led him to the mountain, carrying his sword in one hand and a great leather bag in the other. He stabbed the side of the mountain. There was a rushing, sobbing sound; he clapped his leather bag over the hole, and Ulysses, amazed, saw the great bag flutter and fill. Aeolus held its neck closed, strode to the east face of the mountain, and stabbed again. As the east wind rushed out, he caught it in his sack. Then he stomped to the south slope and stabbed again, and caught the south wind in the sack. Now, very carefully, he wound a silver wire about the neck of the sack. It was full now, swollen, tugging at his arm like a huge leather balloon, trying to fly away.

He said, "In this bag are the north wind, the south wind, and the east wind. You must keep them prisoner. But if you wish to change course—if a pirate should chase you, say, or a sea monster, or if an adventure beckons, then you open the bag very carefully—you and you alone, Captain—and whistle up the wind you wish, let just a breath of it out, close the bag quickly again, and tie it tight. For winds grow swiftly—that is their secret—and so they must be carefully guarded."

"I shall not change course," said Ulysses. "No matter what enemy threatens or what adventure beckons, I sail straight for Ithaca. I shall not open your bag of winds."

"Good," said Aeolus. "Then bind it to your mast, and guard it yourself, sword in hand; let none of your men approach, lest they open it unwittingly. In the meantime, I will send the gentle west wind to follow your ship and fill your sails and take you home."

"Thank you, great Aeolus, thank you, kindly keeper of the winds. I know now that the gods have answered my prayers, and I shall be able to cease this weary, heartbreaking drifting over the face of the sea, having my men killed and eaten, my ships destroyed, and my hopes shattered. I will never cease thanking you, Aeolus, till the day I die."

"May that sad occasion be far off," said Aeolus politely. "Now, sir, much as I like your company, you had better gather your men and be off. I shall be uneasy now until my winds return to me and I can shut them in the mountain again."

Ulysses returned to the castle and called together his men. Gladly they trooped down to the ships and went aboard. Ulysses bound the great leather sack to the mast and warned his crew that no man must touch it on pain of death. Then he himself stood with naked sword under the mast, guarding the sack.

"Up anchor!" he cried.

The west wind rolled off the mountain and filled their sails. The black ships slipped out of the harbor. Away from the island they sailed, away from the mountain and the castle toward the wall of bronze. When they reached the wall, the great gate swung open and they sailed westward over water oily with moonlight. Westward they sailed for nine days and nine nights. In perfect weather they skimmed along, the west wind hovering behind them, keeping their sails full, pushing them steadily home.

And for nine nights and nine days, Ulysses did not sleep; he did not close his eyes or sheath his sword. He kept his station under the mast—food and drink were brought to him there—and never for an instant stopped guarding the sack.

Then, finally, on the morning of the ninth day, he heard the lookout cry, "Land Ho!" and strained his eyes to see. What he saw made his heart swell. Tears coursed down his face, but they were tears of joy. For he saw the dear familiar hills of home. He saw the brown fields of Ithaca, the twisted olive trees, and, as he watched, he saw them even more clearly, saw the white marble columns of his own castle on the cliff. And his men, watching, saw the smoke rising from their own chimneys.

When Ulysses saw the white columns of his palace, he knew that unless the west wind failed, they would be home in an hour, but the friendly wind blew steadily as ever. Ulysses heaved a great sigh. The terrible tension that had kept him awake for nine days and nights eased its grip. He raised his arms and yawned. Then he leaned against the mast and closed his eyes, just for a minute.

Two of the men, standing in the bow, saw him slump at the foot of the mast, fast asleep. Their eyes traveled up the mast to the great leather bag, plump as a balloon, straining against its bonds as the impatient winds wrestled inside. Then Poseidon, swimming invisibly alongside, clinked his golden armlets. The men heard the clinking and thought it came from the bag.

One man said to the other: "Do you hear that? Those are coins, heavy golden coins, clinking against each other. There must be a fortune in that sack."

The other man said, "Yes, a fortune that should belong to all of us by rights. We shared the danger and should share the loot."

"It is true," said the first, "that he has always been generous. He shared the spoils of Troy."

"Yes, but that was then. Why does he not divide this great sack of treasure? Aeolus gave it to him, and we know how rich he is. Aeolus gave it to him as a guest gift, and he should share it with us."

"He never will. Whatever is in that bag, he does not mean for us to see it. Did you not observe how he has been guarding it all these nights and all these days, standing there always, eating and drinking where he stands, never sheathing his sword?"

"It is in his sheath now," said the second sailor. "And his eyes are closed. Look—he sleeps like a babe. I doubt that anything would wake him."

"What are you doing? What are you going to do with that knife? Are you out of your mind?"

"Yes—out of my mind with curiosity, out of my mind with gold fever, if you must know. Ulysses lies asleep. His sword sleeps in its sheath. And I mean to see what is in that bag."

"Wait, I'll help you. But you must give me half."

"Come then. . . ."

Swiftly and silently the two barefooted sailors padded to the mast, slashed the rope that bound the bag to the spar, and bore it away.

"Hurry—open it!"

"I can't. This wire's twisted in a strange knot. Perhaps a magic knot. It won't come out."

"Then we'll do it this way!" cried the sailor with the knife, and struck at the leather bag, slashing it open. He was immediately lifted off his feet and blown like a leaf off the deck and into the sea as the winds rushed howling out of the bag and began to chase each other around the ship. The winds screamed and jeered and laughed, growing, leaping, reveling in their freedom, roaring and squabbling, screeching around and around the ship. They fell on their gentle brother, the west wind, and cuffed him mercilessly until he fled; then they chased each other around the ship again, spinning it like a cork in a whirlpool.

Then, as they heard the far, summoning whistle of the keeper of the winds—far, far to the west on the Aeolian Island—they snarled with rage and roared boisterously homeward, snatching the ships along with them, ripping their sails to shreds, snapping their masts like twigs, and hurling the splintered hulls westward over the boiling sea.

Ulysses awoke from his sleep to find the blue sky black with clouds and his home island dropping far astern, out of sight. He saw his crew flung about the deck like dolls, and the tattered sails and the broken spars, and he did not know whether he was awake or asleep—whether this was some nightmare of loss, or whether he was awake now and had slept before, dreaming a fair dream of home. Whichever it was, he began to understand that he was being made the plaything of great powers.

With the unleashed winds screaming behind him at gale force, the trip back to where they had started took them only two days. And once again the black ships were hurled onto the island of the winds. Ulysses left his crew on the beach and went to the castle. He found Aeolus in his throne room and stood before him, bruised, bloody, clothes torn, eyes like ashes.

"What happened?" cried Aeolus. "Why have you come back?"

"I was betrayed," said Ulysses. "Betrayed by sleep—the most cruel sleep of my life—and then by a wicked, foolish, greedy crew who released the winds from the sack and let us be snatched back from happiness even as we saw the smoke rising from our own chimneys."

"I warned you," said Aeolus. "I warned you not to let anyone touch that bag."

"And you were right, a thousand times right!" cried Ulysses. "Be generous once again. You can heal my woes, you alone. Renew your gift. Lend me the west wind to bear me home again, and I swear to you that this time I shall do everything you bid."

"I can't help you," said Aeolus. "No one can help he whom the gods detest. And they detest you, man—they hate you. What you call bad luck is their hatred, turning gifts into punishment, fair hopes into nightmares. And bad luck is very catching. So please go. Get on your ship and sail away from this island and never return."

"Farewell," said Ulysses, and he strode away.

He gathered his weary men and made them board the ships again. The winds were pent in their mountain. The sea was sluggish. A heavy calm lay over the harbor. They had to row on their broken stumps of oars, crawling like beetles over the gray water. They rowed away from the island, through the bronze gate, and out upon the sullen sea.

And Ulysses, heartbroken, almost dead of grief, tried to hide his feelings from the men; he stood on deck, barking orders, making them mend sail, patch hull, rig new spars, and keep rowing. He took the helm himself and swung the tiller, pointing the bow westward toward home, which, once again, lay at the other end of the sea.

Cannibal Beach

ULYSSES wished to put as much open water as possible between him and the Islands of the Winds, but after six days he realized he would have to put into harbor. His ships were in very poor trim. Their hulls were gashed and splintered, the sails tattered, and the men themselves cut and bruised and half dead with fatigue. It was a terrible punishment his fleet had taken from the brawling winds.

As dusk was thickening they made a landfall. The sight of the island pleased Ulysses; it seemed perfect for his purpose. It had a natural basin of tideless water cupped by a smoothly curved outcropping of rock. And as they sailed through the narrow throat of rock into the harbor they saw a marvelous sight. The purple sky deepened to inky blue, to black, then swiftly paled. Orange bars of fire stood in the sky, then a great flooding of golden light, which purpled again and went dark. Ulysses searched the sky; he had never seen anything like this before. For night followed day upon this island like a hound hunting a deer. The sun chased the moon across the bowl of the sky, and the beach darkened and went light again, moved from bright day to blackest night in the time that it takes to eat a meal.

"This is a wonder," said Ulysses to himself. "And truly, all my life I have sought wonders. But just now I would wish for a more ordinary course of events. All strangeness holds danger now, and we have had our bellyful of adventure for the time. What I pray for now is a space of days without surprise or wild encounter—to have a fair wind and a calm sea and a swift voyage home. Alas, I fear it is not yet to be. I fear this Island of the Racing Sun. And yet I must land here and mend my ships and rest my crew."

The Greek warriors beached their ships and dragged them onto the shore. But according to his prudent custom, Ulysses beached only two ships, keeping one moored in the harbor in the event of attack. Ulysses spoke his orders; the men broke into groups and began to work. Some built fires and began to cook food, others mended sail, some caulked hulls, and sentries kept watch.

"Climb that tall tree there," Ulysses said to one of his men. "Climb to the top and look about, then come down and tell me what you see."

"It's too dark to see," said the sailor.

"You forget where we are," said Ulysses. "Here night chases day, and day pursues night. There will be light enough by the time you reach the top."

The man went off to climb the tree. Ulysses stalked about inspecting the work being done on the ships. The sky paled; dawn bloomed. But the sailor had not returned.

"Odd," said Ulysses. "He must be asleep up there." And he dispatched another sailor to climb the tree to see what happened to the first one.

The shadows were lengthening. The sky shed its gold; shadows yawned and swallowed the light. It was night, and the second sailor had not returned. Ulysses frowned and sent a third man to climb the tree. Then he kept guard there on the beach, in the firelight, eyes narrowed, beard bristling, like a great cat waiting.

The sun minted itself again in the sky; morning flashed. The third sailor had not returned. Ulysses decided to climb the tree himself. It was a good half-mile from where he stood, a huge solitary tree stretching up, up. When he reached it he saw that its bark was wrinkled in a most curious way; it fell in soft brown folds unlike any bark he had ever seen. And when he grasped the tree to climb it, the bark felt like a heavy cloth beneath his hands. But it made climbing easy. Up and up he went; up, up in the thickening darkness, climbing with the ease of a man of the Middle Sea who had begun to climb masts as soon as he could walk.

He climbed and climbed, rested, and climbed again. Suddenly he heard a mumbling, chuckling sound as if some beast were crouching in the branches above. He stopped climbing and peered upward. He could see no branches. Reaching up he felt a hairy foliage grazing his fingers. He clung there to the branch, right where he was, not moving, until the blackness thinned, and he began to see.

He had been climbing through darkness; now he saw against the paler sky toward what he had been climbing. The hairy foliage was a beard. A huge bushy beard, hanging some forty feet above the ground. Above that beard was a grinning of enormous teeth; above the teeth the muddy gleam of eyes as large as portholes. Ulysses' head swam with fear. Fear pried at his legs and arms, and he had to clutch the trunk with all his strength to keep from falling. But it was no trunk. He had been climbing no tree. It was a giant's leg he had been climbing, and the clothlike bark was cloth indeed, the stuff of its garment. And he realized then that the three sailors he had sent aloft had climbed to a mumbling death.

Ulysses thanked the gods then that he had begun his climb in darkness, for he understood that the giant slept standing, like a horse, and that his eyes were not yet adjusted to the new light. That is why the huge slab of hand he saw swinging there now had not trapped him like a fly. He loosened his grasp and slid down so swiftly that he tore the skin off his hands. But he was mindless of pain. He hit the ground and raised a great shout. "To the ships!" he cried. "To the ships!"

But it was too late. The sun was burning in the sky and there was too much light. A brutal bellowing yell shattered the air, and the men, paralyzed with fear, whimpering like puppies, saw a mob of giants, tall as trees, trooping toward them over the hills. And before Ulysses could rally his terrified men, the giants were upon them, trampling the ships like twigs, scooping the men up and popping them into their mouths like children eating berries.

Ulysses did not lose his wits. Fear turned to anger in him, and anger became an icy flame that quickened him. His sword was scything the air; he hacked away at the giant hands that came at him like a flock of huge meaty gulls. He whipped his blade at their fingers, hacking them off at the knuckle joints. His sword smoked with blood.

Inspired by the sight of him fencing with the giant fingers, a small group of his men gathered around and made a hedge of steel. They hacked their way through the great grasping hands to the edge of the sea, then followed Ulysses into the water and swam to the single ship that they had left moored in the harbor. Luckily the swift night was falling again, and they were shielded by darkness. They heard the huge snuffling noise of the giants feasting upon their shipmates, but there was nothing they could do except try to save themselves. The night had brought an off-shore wind. Swiftly they raised sail and darted through the throat of rock out into the open sea.

Of the three ships that had gone in, only one sailed away. Of the three crews but one was left. The others had gone down the gullets of the giants who lived on that strange island where night hounds the golden stag of the day across the indifferent sky.

Circe

NOW, after battling the giant cannibals on the Island of the Racing Sun, Ulysses found himself with only forty-five men left from his crew of one hundred. He was determined to bring these men home safely or die himself.

They were sailing northward again, and on the third day came in sight of land, low-lying, heavily wooded, with a good sheltering harbor. Although they had met terrible treatment everywhere they had landed since leaving Troy, they were out of food, water was running low, and once again they would have to risk the perils of the land.

Ulysses was very cautious. He moored the ship offshore and said to the crew:

"I shall go ashore myself—alone—to see what there is to see and make sure there are no terrible hosts, giants, man-eating ogres, or secret sorceries. If I am not back by nightfall, Eury-lochus will act as captain. Then he will decide whether to seek food and water here or sail onward. Farewell."

He lowered a small boat and rowed toward the island, all alone. He beached his skiff and struck inland. The first thing he wanted to do was find out whether he was on an island, or the spur of a mainland. He climbed a low hill, then climbed to the top of a tree that grew on the hill. He was high enough now for a clear view, and he turned slowly, marking the flash of the sea on all sides. He knew that once again they had landed on an is-land and that the ship was their only means of escape if danger should strike.

Something caught his eye. He squinted thoughtfully at what looked like a feather of smoke rising from a grove of trees. The trees were too thick for him to see through. He climbed down and picked his way carefully toward the smoke, trying to make

as little noise as possible. He came to a stand of mighty trees—
oak trees, thick and tall with glossy leaves. Glimmering through
the trees he saw what looked like a small castle made of polished gray stone. He did not dare go near, for he heard strange
howling sounds, a pack of dogs, perhaps, but different from any
dogs he had ever heard. So he left the grove and made his way
back toward the beach, thinking hard, trying to decide whether
to sail away immediately or take a chance on the inhabitants
being friendly. He did not like the sound of that howling. There
was something in it that froze his marrow. He decided that he
would not risk his men on the island but that he would return
to the ship, raise anchor, and sail away to seek food elsewhere.

Just then a tall white deer with mighty antlers stepped across
his path. The great stag had a bearing proud as a king and did
not deign to run but walked on haughtily as if he knew no one
would dare to attack him. Unfortunately for the stag, however,
Ulysses was too hungry to be impressed by any animal's own
opinion of himself. The warrior raised his bronze spear and flung
it with all the power of his knotted arm. It sang through the air,
pierced the stag's body, and nailed him to a tree. The stag died
standing up, still in his pride. He was a huge animal, so large that
Ulysses feared he could not carry him back to the ship unaided.
But then he remembered how hungry his men were, and he decided to try. He picked weeds and wove a rope, which he twisted
and twisted again until it was as strong as a ship's line. Then he
bound the stag's legs together, swung the great carcass up onto
his back, and staggered off using his spear as a cane.

He was at the end of his strength when he reached the beach
and let the deer slip to the sand. He signaled to his men, who left
the ship moored and came ashore on five small boats. They raised
a mighty shout of joy when they saw the dead stag. All hands fell
to. In a twinkling the deer was skinned and cut up. Fires were
lighted, and the delicious smell of roasting meat drew the gulls to
the beach, screaming and dipping, begging for scraps.

The men gorged themselves, then lay on the sand to sleep.
Ulysses, himself, kept guard. All that night he stood watch,
leaning on his spear, looking at the moon, which hung in the
sky like an orange and paled as it climbed. As he watched, he
turned things over in his mind, trying to decide what to do.
While he was still bothered by the eerie howling of the mysterious animals at the castle, still, with his belly full, he felt less
gloomy. The more he thought about it the wiser it seemed to explore the island thoroughly and try to determine whether it was

a friendly place or not. For never before had he seen a deer so large. If there was one, there must be more; and with game like that the ship could be provisioned in a few days. Also the island was full of streams from which they could fill their dry casks with pure water.

"Yes," he said to himself, "perhaps our luck has changed. Perhaps the god that was playing with us so spitefully has found other amusements. Yes, we will explore this island and see what there is to see."

Next morning he awakened his men and divided them into two groups, one led by himself, the other by Eurylochus. He said to Eurylochus: "There is a castle on this island. We must find out who lives there. If he be friendly, or not too strong a foe, we will stay here and hunt and lay in water until the hold be full; then we will depart. Now choose, Eurylochus. Would you rather stay here with your men and guard the ship while I visit the castle—or would you rather I keep the beach? Choose."

"O Ulysses," Eurylochus said. "I am sick of the sight of the sea. Even as my belly hungers for food, so do my eyes hunger for leaves and trees which might recall our dear Ithaca. And my foot longs to tread something more solid than a deck—a floor that does not pitch and toss and roll. Pray, gentle Ulysses, let me and my men try the castle."

"Go," said Ulysses. "May the gods go with you."

So Eurylochus and twenty-two men set out, while Ulysses guarded the ship. As the band of warriors approached the castle, they too heard a strange howling. Some of them drew their swords. Others notched arrows to their bowstrings. They pressed on, preparing to fight. They passed through the grove of oak trees and came to where the trees thinned. Here the howling grew louder and wilder. Then, as they passed the last screen of trees and came to the courtyard of the shining gray castle, they saw an extraordinary sight—a pack of wolves and lions running together like dogs—racing about the courtyard, howling.

When they caught sight of the men, the animals turned and flung themselves upon the strangers, so swiftly that no man had time to use his weapon. The great beasts stood on their hind legs and put their forepaws on the men's shoulders, and fawned on them and licked their faces. They voiced low, muttering, growling whines. Eurylochus, who stood half-embracing a huge tawny lion, said, "Men, it is most strange. For these fearsome beasts greet us as though we were lost friends. They seem to be trying to speak to us. And look—look— at their eyes! How intelligently they gleam, how sadly they gaze. Not like beasts' eyes at all."

"It is true," said one of the men. "But perhaps there is nothing to fear. Perhaps there is reason to take heart. For if wild beasts are so tame and friendly, then perhaps the master of the castle, whoever he is or whatever he is, will be friendly too, and welcome us, and give us good cheer."

"Come," said Eurylochus.

When they reached the castle gate, they stopped and listened. For they heard a woman singing in a lovely, deep, full-throated voice, so that without seeing the woman they knew she was beautiful.

Eurylochus said, "Men, you go into the castle and see what is to be seen. I will stay here and make sure you are not surprised."

"What do you mean? You come with us. Listen to that. There can be no danger where there is such song."

"Yes, everything seems peaceful," said Eurylochus. "The wild animals are friendly. Instead of the clank of weapons, we hear a woman singing. And it may be peaceful. But something says to me, be careful, take heed. Go you, then. I stay on guard. If I am attacked, and you are unharmed, come to my aid. If anything happens to you, then I shall take word back to Ulysses."

So Eurylochus stood watch at the castle gate—sword in one hand, dagger in the other, bow slung across his back—and the rest of the men entered the castle. They followed the sound of singing through the rooms and out onto a sunny terrace. There sat a woman weaving. She sat at a huge loom, larger than they had ever seen, and wove a gorgeous tapestry. As she wove, she sang. The bright flax leaped through her fingers as if it were dancing to the music in her voice. The men stood and stared. The sun seemed to be trapped in her hair, so bright it was; she wore it long, falling to her waist. Her dress was as blue as the summer sky, matching her eyes. Her long white arms were bare to the shoulders. She stood up and greeted them. She was very tall. And the men, looking at her and listening to her speak, began to believe that they were in the presence of a goddess.

She seemed to read thoughts, too, for she said, "No, I am not a goddess. But I am descended from the Immortals. I am Circe, granddaughter of Helios, a sun-god, who married Perse, daughter of Oceanus. So what am I—wood nymph, sea nymph, something of both? Or something more? I can do simple magic and prophesy, weave certain homely enchantments, and read dreams. But let us not speak of me, but of you, strangers. You are adventurers, I see, men of the sword, men of the black-prowed ships, the hawks of the sea. And you have come through sore, sad times and seek a haven here on this western isle. So be it. I welcome you. For the sweetest spell Circe weaves is one called hospitality. I will have baths drawn for you, clean garments laid out. And when you are refreshed, you shall come and dine. For I love brave men and the tales they tell."

When the men had bathed and changed, Circe gave them each a red bowl. And into each bowl she put yellow food—a kind of porridge made of cheese, barley, honey, and wine plus a few secret things known only to herself. The odor that rose from the red bowls was more delicious than anything they had ever smelled before. And as each man ate, he felt himself sinking into his hunger, *becoming* his hunger—lapping, panting, grunting, snuffling. Circe passed among them, smiling, filling the bowls again and again. And the men, waiting for their bowls to be filled, looking about, seeing each other's faces smeared with food, thought, "How strange. We're eating like pigs."

Even as the thought came, it became more true. For as Circe passed among them now she touched each one on the shoulder with a wand, saying: "Glut and swink, eat and drink, gobble food and guzzle wine. Too rude, I think, for humankind, quite right, I think, for *swine!*"

As she said these words in her lovely, laughing voice, the men dwindled. Their noses grew wide and long, became snouts. Their hair hardened into bristles; their hands and feet became hooves, and they ran about on all fours, sobbing and snuffling, searching the floor for bones and crumbs. But all the time they cried real tears from their little red eyes, for they were pigs only in form; their minds remained unchanged, and they knew what was happening to them.

Circe kicked them away from the table. "To the sties!" she cried. She struck them with her wand, herding them out of the castle into a large sty. And there she flung them acorns and chestnuts and red berries and watched them grubbing in the mud for the food she threw. She laughed a wild, bright laugh and went back into the castle.

While all this was happening, Eurylochus was waiting at the gate. When the men did not return he crept up to a bow slit in the castle wall and looked in. It was dark now. He saw the glimmer of torchlight and the dim shape of a woman at a loom, weaving. He heard a voice singing, the same enchanting voice he had heard before. But of his men he saw nothing. Nor did he hear their voices. A great fear seized him. He raced off as fast as he could, hoping against hope that the beasts would not howl. The wolves and lions stood like statues, walked like shadows. Their eyes glittered with cold moonlight, but none of them uttered a sound.

He ran until the breath strangled in his throat, until his heart tried to crack out of his ribs, but he kept running, stumbling over roots, slipping on stones. He ran and ran until he reached the beach and fell swooning in Ulysses' arms. Then with his last breath he gasped out the story, told Ulysses of the lions and the wolves, of the woman singing in the castle, and how the men had gone in and not come out. And then he slipped into blackness.

Ulysses said to his men: "You hear the story Eurylochus tells. I must go to the castle and see what has happened to your companions. But there is no need for you to risk yourselves. You stay here. And if I do not return by sunfall tomorrow, then you must board the ship and sail away, for you will know that I am dead."

The men wept and pleaded with him not to go, but he said: "I have sworn an oath that I will never leave another man behind if there is any way I can prevent it. Farewell, dear friends."

It was dawn by the time he found himself among the oak trees near the castle. He heard the first faint howling of the animals in the courtyard. And as he walked through the rose and gray light, a figure started up before him—a slender youth in golden breastplates and a golden hat with wings on it, holding a golden staff. Ulysses fell to his knees.

"Why do you kneel, venerable sir?" said the youth. "You are older than I, and a mighty warrior. You should not kneel."

"Ah, pardon," cried Ulysses. "I have sharp eyes for some things. Behind your youth—so fair—I see time itself stretching to the beginning of things. Behind your slenderness I sense the power of a god. Sweet youth, beautiful lad, I know you. You are Hermes, the swift one, the messenger god. I pray you have come with good tidings for me, because I fear that I have offended the gods, or one of them anyway, and he has vowed vengeance upon me."

"It is true," said Hermes. "Somebody up there doesn't like you. Can't say who, not ethical, you know. But if you *should* suspect that he may have something to do with the management of sea matters, well, you're a good guesser, that's all."

"Poseidon . . . I have offended Poseidon," muttered Ulysses, "the terrible one, the earth shaker."

"Well," said Hermes, "what do you expect? That unpleasant Cyclops whom you first blinded, then taunted, is Poseidon's son, you know. Not a son to be proud of, but blood is thicker than water, as they say, even in the god of the sea. So Polyphemus tattled to his father and asked him to do dreadful things to you, which, I'm afraid, he's been doing. Now, this castle you're going to is Circe's and she is a very dangerous person to meet—a sorceress, a doer of magical mischief. And she is waiting for you, Ulysses. She sits at her loom, weaving, waiting. For you. She has already entertained your shipmates. Fed them. Watched them making pigs of themselves. And, finally, she helped them on their way a bit. In brief, they are now in a sty, being fattened. And one day they will make a most excellent meal for someone not too fussy. Among Circe's guests are many peculiar feeders."

"Thunder and lightning!" cried Ulysses. "What can I do!"

"Listen and learn," said Hermes. "I have come to help you. Poseidon's wrath does not please all of us, you know. We gods have our moods, and they're not always kind, but somehow or other we must keep things balanced. And so I have come to help you. You must do exactly as I say, or nothing can help you. Now listen closely. First, take this."

He snapped his fingers and a flower appeared between them. It was white and heavily scented, with a black and yellow root. He gave it to Ulysses.

"It is called *moly*," he said. "It is magical. So long as you carry it, Circe's drugs will not work. You will go to the castle. She will greet you and feed you. You will eat the food which, to her amazement, will leave you unharmed. Then you will draw your sword and advance upon her as though you meant to kill her. Then she will see that you have certain powers and will begin to plead with you. She will unveil enchantments more powerful than any she has yet used. Resist them you cannot, nor can any man, nor any god. Nor is there any counterspell that will work against such beauty. But if you wish to see your home again, if you wish to rescue your shipmates from the sty, you must resist her long enough to make her swear the great oath of the immortals—that she will not do you any harm as long as you are her guest. That is all I can do for you. From now on, it is up to you. We shall be watching you with interest. Farewell."

The golden youth disappeared just as a ray of sunlight does when a cloud crosses the face of the sun. Ulysses shook his head, wondering whether he had really seen the god or imagined him, but then he saw that he was still holding the curious flower, and he knew that Hermes had indeed been there. So he marched on toward the castle, through the pack of lions and wolves, who leaped about him, fawning, looking at him with their great intelligent eyes and trying to warn him in their snarling, growling voices. He stroked their heads, passed among them, and went into the castle.

And here, he found Circe, sitting at her loom, weaving and singing. She wore a white tunic now and a flame-colored scarf and was as beautiful as the dawn. She stood up and greeted him, saying:

"Welcome, stranger. I live here alone and seldom see anyone and almost never have guests. So you are triply welcome, great sea-stained warrior, for I know that you have seen battle and adventure and have tales to tell."

She drew him a warm, perfumed bath, and her servants bathed and anointed him and gave him clean garments to wear. When he came to her, she gave him a red bowl full of yellow food and said, "Eat." The food smelled delicious; its fragrance was intoxicating. Ulysses felt that he wanted to plunge his face into it and grub it up like a pig, but he held the flower tightly, kept control of himself, and ate slowly. He did not quite finish the food.

"Delicious," he said. "Your own recipe?"

"Yes," she said. "Will you not finish?"

"I am not quite so hungry as I thought."

"Then drink. Here's wine."

She turned her back to him as she poured the wine, and he knew that she was casting a powder in it. He smiled to himself and drank off the wine, then said: "Delicious. Your own grapes?"

"You look weary, stranger," she said. "Sit and talk with me."

"Gladly," said Ulysses. "We have much to speak of, you and I. I'm something of a farmer myself. I breed cattle on my own little island of Ithaca, where I'm king—when I'm home. Won't you show me your livestock?"

"Livestock? I keep no cattle here."

"Oh, do you not? I fancied I heard pigs squealing out there. Must have been mistaken."

"Yes," said Circe. "Badly mistaken."

"But you do have interesting animals. I was much struck by the wolves and lions who course in a pack like dogs—very friendly for such savage beasts."

"I have taught them to be friendly," said Circe. "I am friendly myself, you see, and I like all the members of my household to share my goodwill."

"Their eyes," said Ulysses. "I was struck by their eyes—so big and sad and clever. You know, as I think of it, they looked like . . . human eyes."

"Did they?" said Circe. "Well—the eyes go last."

She came to him swiftly, raised her wand, touched him on the shoulder, and said: "Change, change, change! Turn, turn, turn!"

Nothing happened. Her eyes widened when she saw him sitting there, unchanged, sniffing at the flower he had taken from his tunic. He took the wand from her gently and snapped it in two. Then drawing his sword, he seized her by her long golden hair and forced her to her knees, pulling her head until her white throat was offered the blade of the sword. Then he said: "You have not asked me my name. It is Ulysses. I am an unlucky man but not altogether helpless. You have changed my men into pigs. Now I will change you into a corpse."

She did not flinch before the blade. Her great blue eyes looked into his. She took the sharp blade in her hand, stroked it gently, and said: "It is almost worth dying to be overcome by so mighty a warrior. But I think living might be interesting, too, now that I have met you."

He felt her fingers burning the cold metal of the sword as if the blade had become part of his body. He tried to turn his head but sank deeper into the blueness of her eyes.

"Yes, I am a sorceress," she murmured, "a wicked woman. But you are a sorcerer, too, are you not? Changing me more than I have changed your men, for I changed only their bodies and you have changed my soul. It is no longer a wicked plotting soul but soft and tender and womanly, full of love for you."

Her voice throbbed. She stroked the sword blade. He raised her to her feet and said:

"You are beautiful enough to turn any man into an animal. I will love you. But even before I am a man, I am a leader. My men are my responsibility. Before we can love each other I must ask you to swear the great oath that you will not harm me when I am defenseless, that you will not wound me and suck away my blood as witches do, but will treat me honestly, and that, first of all, you will restore my men to their own forms and let me take them with me when I am ready to leave."

"I will try to see that you are never ready," said Circe softly.

Circe kept her promise. The next morning she took Ulysses out to the sty and called the pigs. They came trotting up, snuffing and grunting. As they streamed past her, rushing to Ulysses, she touched each one on the shoulder with her wand. As she did so, each pig stood up, his hind legs grew longer, his front hooves became hands, his eyes grew, his nose shrank, his quills softened into hair, and he was his human self once more, only grown taller and younger.

The men crowded around Ulysses, shouting and laughing. He said to them: "Welcome, my friends. You have gone a short but ugly voyage to the animal state. And while you have returned—looking very well—it is clear that we are in a place of sorceries and must conduct ourselves with great care. Our enchanting hostess, Circe, has become so fond of our company that she insists we stay awhile. This, indeed, is the price of your release from hogdom. So you will now go down to your shipmates on the beach and tell them what has happened. Ask them to secure the ship and then return here with you to the castle. It is another delay in our journey, but it is far better than what might have been. Go, then."

The men trooped happily down to the harbor and told the others what had happened. At first, Eurylochus protested. "How do I know," he said, "that you are not still under enchantment? How do I know that this is not some new trick of the sorceress to get us all into her power, turn us all to pigs, and keep us in the sty forever?"

But the other men paid no heed to his warning. They were eager to see the castle and the beautiful witch, to taste the delicious food, and enjoy all the luxuries their friends had described. So they obeyed Ulysses' commands. They dragged the ship up on the beach, beyond reach of the tide, unstepped its mast, then marched off laughing and singing toward the castle, carrying mast and oars and folded sail. Eurylochus followed, but he was afraid.

For some time, things went well. Ulysses and Circe lived as husband and wife. The men were treated as welcome guests. They feasted for hours each night in the great dining hall. And as they ate, they were entertained by minstrels singing, by acrobats, dancing bears, and dancing girls. During the day they swam in the ocean, hunted wild boar, threw the discus, had archery and spear-throwing contests, raced, jumped, and wrestled. Then as dusk drew in they returned to the castle for their warm, perfumed baths and bowls of hot wine before the feasting began again.

As for Ulysses, he found himself falling deeper under Circe's spell every day. Thoughts of home were dim now. He barely remembered his wife's face. Sometimes he would think of days gone by and wonder when he could shake off this enchantment and resume his voyage. Then she would look at him. And her eyes, like blue flame, burned these pictures out of his head. Then he could not rest until he was within the scent of her hair, the touch of her hand. And he would whimper impatiently like a dog dreaming, shake his head, and go to her.

"It is most curious," she said. "But I love you more than all my other husbands."

"In the name of heaven, how many have you had?" he cried.

"Ah, don't say it like that. Not so many, when you consider. I have been a frequent widow, it is true. But, please understand, I am god-descended on both sides. I am immortal and cannot die. I have lived since the beginning of things."

"Yes. How many husbands have you had?"

"Please, my dear, be fair. Gods have loved me, and satyrs and fauns and centaurs, and other creatures who do not die. But I, I have always had a taste for humankind. My favorite husbands have been men, human men. They, you see, grow old so quickly, and I am alone again. And time grows heavy and breeds mischief."

"How many husbands have you buried, dear widow?"

"Buried? Why, none."

"I see. You cremate them."

"I do not let them die. I cannot bear dead things. Especially if they are things I have loved. Of all nature's transformations, death seems to me the most stupid. No, I do not let them die. I change them into animals, and they roam this beautiful island forevermore. And I see them every day and feed them with my own hand."

"That explains those wolves and lions in the courtyard, I suppose."

"Ah, they are only the best, the cream, the mightiest warriors of ages gone. But I have had lesser husbands. They are now rabbits, squirrels, boars, cats, spiders, frogs, and monkeys. That little fellow there"—she pointed to a silvery little ape who was prancing and gibbering on top of the bedpost—"he who pelts you with walnut shells every night. He was very jealous, very busy and jealous, and still is. I picked their forms, you see, to match their dispositions. Is it not thoughtful of me?"

"Tell me," said Ulysses, "when I am used up, will I be good enough to join your select band of wolves and lions, or will I be something less? A toad, perhaps, or a snail?"

"A fox, undoubtedly," she said. "With your swiftness and your cunning ways—oh, yes, a fox. A king of foxes." She stroked his beard. "But you are the only man who ever withstood my spells," she said. "You are my conqueror, a unique hero. It is not your fate to stay with me. It is not my happy fate to arrange your last hours."

"Is it not?" said Ulysses.

"No," she said. "Unless you can wipe out of your mind all thoughts of home. Unless you can erase all dreams of battle and voyage, unless you can forget your men and release me from my oath and let them become animals, contented animals, then and then only, can you remain with me as husband forever. And I will give you of my immortality. Yes, that can be arranged. I know how. You will share my immortality and live days of sport and idleness and nights of love. And we will live together always, knowing no other, and we will never grow old."

"Can such a thing be?"

"Yes. But the decision is yours. I have sworn an oath and cannot keep you against your will. If you choose, you can remain here with me and make this island a paradise of pleasure. If not, you must resume your voyage and encounter dangers more dreadful than any you have seen yet. You will watch friends dying before your eyes, have your own life imperiled a hundred times, be battered, bruised, torn, wave-tossed, all this, if you leave me. But it is for you to decide."

Ulysses stood up and strode to the edge of the terrace. From where he stood he could see the light dancing in a million hot little needles on the blue water. In the courtyard he saw the wolves and the lions. Beyond the courtyard, at the edge of the wood, he saw his men, happy-looking, healthy, tanned; some were wrestling, some flinging spears, others drawing the bow. Circe had crossed to her loom and was weaving, weaving and singing. He remembered his wife. She also, at home in Ithaca, would sit and weave. But how different she looked. Her hair was no fleece of burning gold, but black. She was much smaller than Circe, and she did not sing.

"I have decided," he said. "I must go."

"Must you?"

"Yes."

"First let me tell you what the gods have decreed. If you sail away from this island, you cannot head for home. First you must go to the Land of the Dead."

"The Land of the Dead?" cried Ulysses. "No! No! It cannot be!"

"To the Land of the Dead. To Tartarus. This is the decree. You must go there with all your men. And there you must consult certain ghosts, of whom you will be told, and they will prophesy for you and plan your homeward journey. And theirs is the route you must follow if you wish to see Ithaca again."

"The Land of the Dead, dark Tartarus, the realm of torment from which no mortal returns. Must I go there?"

"Unless you stay with me here, in peace, in luxury, in every pleasure but that of adventure."

"It cannot be," said Ulysses. "As you, beautiful sorceress, choose a form for your lovers that matches their natures and which they must wear when they are no longer men, so the Fates, with their shears, have cut out my destiny. It is danger, toil, battle, uncertainty. And, though I stop and refresh myself now and again, still must I resume my voyage, for that is my nature. And to fit my nature has fate cut the pattern of my days."

"Go quickly," said Circe. "Call your men and depart. For if you stay here any longer, I shall forget all duty. I shall break my oath and keep you here by force and never let you go. Quickly then, brave one, quickly!"

Ulysses summoned his men and led them down to the beach. They stepped the mast, rigged the sails, and sailed away. They caught a northwest puff. The sails filled and the black ship ran out of the harbor. Ulysses' face was wet with Circe's last tears and his heart was very heavy. But then spray dashed into his face with the old remembered bright shock, and he laughed.

The last sound the men heard as the ship threaded through the mouth of the harbor and ran for the open sea was the howling of the lions and wolves who had followed them down to the beach. They stood now breast-deep in the surf, gazing after the white sail, crying their loneliness.

The Land of the Dead

IN those days men knew that the Ocean Stream was a huge river girdling the earth. Hades' kingdom, dark Tartarus, was presumed to be on the farther shore, over the edge of the visible world. But no one could be certain, for those who went there did not return.

Now it had been foretold by Circe that Ulysses would have to visit the Land of the Dead and be advised by wise ghosts before he could resume his journey and find his way back to Ithaca. So he turned his bow westward; and a strong east wind caught his white sails and sent the ship skimming toward waters no ship had sailed before.

Night tumbled from the sky and set its blackness on the sea and would not lift. The ship sailed blindly. The men were clamped in a nameless grief. They could hardly bear the sound of their own voices but spoke to each other in whispers. The night wore on and did not give way to dawn. There were no stars, no moon. They sailed westward and waited for dawn, but no crack of light appeared in the sky. The darkness would not lift.

Once again Ulysses lashed himself to the tiller and stuck splinters of wood in his eye sockets to prop the weary lids. And, finally, after a week of night, a feeble light did curdle the sky— not a regular dawn, no joyous burst of sun, but a grudging milky grayness that floated down and thickened into fog. Still Ulysses did not dare to sleep, for day was no better than night; no man could see in the dense woolly folds of fog.

Still the east wind blew, pushing them westward through the curdling mist, and still Ulysses did not dare give over the helm. For he had heard that the westward rim of the world was always fog-girt, and was studded by murderously rocky islets, where dwelt the Cimmerians, who waited quietly in the fog for ships to crack upon their shores and deliver to them their natural food, shipwrecked sailors. Finally, Ulysses knew he could not keep awake any longer; yet he knew too that to give over the helm to anyone else meant almost certain death for them all. So he sent a sailor named Elpenor to climb the mast and try to see some distance ahead. No sooner had Elpenor reached the top of the mast than the ship yawed sharply. Ulysses lost his footing and stumbled against the mast.

No one saw Elpenor fall. The fog was too thick. But they heard his terrible scream turned into a choking gurgle. And they knew that he had been shaken from the mast and had fallen into the sea and been drowned. No sooner had his voice gone still than the fog thinned. They could see from one end of the ship to the other—the wet sails, the shining spar, each other's wasted faces. A white gull rose screaming and flew ahead of them.

"Follow that gull," said Ulysses. "He will lead us where we must go."

Then he stretched himself on the deck and went to sleep. Whereupon the crew began to whisper among themselves that the gull was the spirit of their shipmate, Elpenor, and that Ulysses had shaken him from the mast purposely, as one shakes fruit from a tree, so that he might fall in the water and be drowned, giving them the white flight of his spirit to follow to Tartarus.

"He has murdered our shipmate," they whispered to each other, "as he will murder us all to gain his ends."

But they did not dare say it loud enough to awaken Ulysses.

All day they sailed, following the white flash of the gull, and when night came there were no stars and no moon, nothing but choking blackness. Ulysses took the helm again. But now the bow tipped forward and the stern arose, and the ship slipped through the water with a rushing, rustling speed as if it were sailing downhill. The men clung to the shrouds and wept, groaned, and pleaded with Ulysses to change course. But he answered them not at all. He planted his feet and gripped the tiller with all his strength, as the deck tilted and the ship slipped down, down. . . .

"Who has ever heard of the sea sloping?" he said to himself. "Truly this must be the waterway to the underworld, and we are the first keel to cut these fathoms. May the gods grant we cross them again going the other way."

There was a roaring of waters. The deck leveled. They sailed out of darkness as through a curtain and found themselves in a strange place. The sea had narrowed to a river, the water was black, and the sky was black, curving downward like the inside of a bowl; the light was gray. Tall trees grew along the bank of the river—black poplars and white birches. And Ulysses knew that the black river was the Styx, and that he had sailed his ship into the Kingdom of the Dead.

There was no wind, but the sails remained strangely taut, and the ship floated easily into harbor, as if some invisible hand had taken the helm.

Ulysses bade his men disembark. He led them past a fringe of trees to a great meadow where black goats cropped black grass. He drew his sword and scraped out a shallow trench, then had his men cut the throats of two black goats and hold them over the trench until it was filled with blood. For it was ghosts he had come to counsel with, and ghosts, he knew, came only where they could find fresh blood to drink, hoping always to fill their dry veins.

The meadow was still. No birds sang. There was no shrill of insects; the goats did not bleat. The men were too frightened to breathe. Ulysses waited, leaning on his sword, gloomily watching the trench of blood. Then he heard a rustling and saw the air thicken into spouts of steam. Steamy shapes separated, heads and shoulders of mist leaning over the trench to drink, growing more solid as they drank.

One raised its head and looked at him. He shuddered. It was his mother, Anticleia.

"Greetings, Mother. How do you fare?"

"Poorly, son. I am dead, dead, dead. I kept telling you I would die one day, but you never believed me. Now you see. But do you see? Say you see."

A thin tittering arose from the ghosts, and they spoke in steamy whispers.

"What are you doing here, man? You're still alive. Go and die properly and come back, and we will welcome you."

"Silence!" cried Ulysses. "I come for better counsel than this. I must find my way back to Ithaca past the mighty wrath of a god who reaches his strong hand and swirls the sea as a child does a mud puddle, dashing my poor twig of a ship from peril to grim peril. I need good counsel to get home. Where is the sage, Teiresias? Why is he not here to greet me?"

"Coming—coming—He is blind but he smells blood as far as any."

"Do not drink it all. Save some for him."

And Ulysses smote the ghosts with his sword, driving them back, whimpering, from the trench of blood.

But then, striding across the meadow, came certain ghosts in armor. Ulysses bowed low.

"Welcome, O Fox of War," cried the ghost of Achilles. "Tell me, do men remember me in Arcadia?"

"The gods have not allowed me to set foot upon our dear islands," said Ulysses. "But on whatever savage shore I am thrown there are those who know the name of great Achilles. Your fame outshines all warriors who have ever handled weapons. And your son, Neoptolemus, is a hero, too."

"Thank you, Ulysses," said the ghost of Achilles. "Your words are fair and courteous, as always. Now, heed this: When you leave this place, you will sail past an island where you will hear the voices of maidens singing. And the sound of their singing will be sweeter than memories of home, and when your men hear them, their wits will be scattered, and they will wish to dive overboard and swim to shore. If they do, they will perish. For these maidens are a band of witch sisters—music-mad sisters—who lure sailors to the rocks so that they may flay them and make drums of their skin and flutes of their bones. They are the Siren sisters. When you pass their shore, steer clear, steer clear."

"Thank you, great Achilles."

Next to Achilles stood a huge ghost staring at Ulysses out of empty eye sockets. He was a giant skeleton. He wore a cloak of stiffened blood and a red plume upon his skull. His spear and sword were made of bone, too. He was Ajax.

"You tricked me, Ulysses," he said. "When great Achilles here fell on the field of battle, you claimed his golden armor by craft, when I should have had it, I . . . I . . . You took the golden armor that my heart desired and drove me mad with rage, so that I butchered cattle and captives, and then killed myself. I hate you, sly one, and have this bad news for you: If you ever do reach Ithaca, you will find your wife being courted by other men, your son a captive in your own castle, your substance devoured. This is my word to you, Ulysses. So you had simply better fall on your sword now where you stand and save another trip to Hades."

"Thank you, great Ajax," said Ulysses. "I will remember what you have told me."

"I knew that Penelope was being wooed by other men in your absence," said Ulysses' mother. "I knew it well, but I would not speak evil of your wife, not I, not I. . . ."

"Thank you, Mother," said Ulysses.

Then came a ghost so new that his flesh had not quite turned to mist but quivered on his bones like a pale jelly. He was Elpenor, who had fallen from the mast and had led them to Tartarus. When Ulysses saw who it was, he was taken by a great dread and cried, "I did not push you, Elpenor. You fell. It was an accident, I swear."

"Nevertheless," said Elpenor, "my ghost will trouble you until you make my grave."

"How will I do that?"

"The first land you come to, build me a barrow and set thereon my oar. If you forget, I shall scratch at your windows and howl down your chimney and dance in your sleep."

"I will build your grave with my own hands," said Ulysses. "Have you any counsel for me?"

"Yes. Death has cleared my eyes, and I see things I would not have known. I see your ship now sailing in a narrow place between two huge rocks. Beneath the starboard rock is a cave, and in that cave squats Scylla, an unpleasant lady with twelve legs and six heads who cries with the voice of a newborn puppy. If you sail too near that rock, she will seize six sailors to feed her six mouths—"

"Then I will steer away from Scylla—toward the other rock."

"Ah, but under the other rock lurks a strange, thirsty monster named Charybdis, whose habit it is to drink up a whole tide of water in one gulp, and then spit it out again, making a whirlpool of such terrible sucking force that any ship within its swirl must be destroyed."

"Monster to the right and monster to the left," cried Ulysses. "What can I do then?"

"You must keep to the middle way. But if you cannot—and indeed it will be very difficult, for you will be tacking against headwinds—then choose the right-hand rock where hungry Scylla squats. For it is better to lose six men than your ship and your entire crew."

"Thank you, courteous Elpenor," said Ulysses. "I will heed your words."

Then the air grew vaporous as the mob of ghosts shifted and swayed, making way for one who cleaved forward toward the trench of blood, and Ulysses recognized the one he was most eager to see, the blind woman-shaped ghost of Teiresias, sage of Thebes, expert at disasters, master of prophecy.

"Hail, venerable Teiresias," he cried, "all honor to you. I have journeyed far to make your acquaintance."

Teiresias came silently to the trench, knelt, and drank. He drank until the trench was empty and the misty bladder of his body was faintly pink.

"You honor me by your visit, Ulysses," he said. "Many men sought my counsel when I was alive, but you are the first client to make his way down here. You have heard these others tell you of certain petty dangers that you will do well to avoid, but I have a mighty thing to tell."

"Tell."

"Your next landfall will be a large island that men shall one day call Sicily. Here the Sun-Titan, Hyperion, pastures his herds of golden cattle. Your stores will have been eaten when you reach this place, and your men will be savage with hunger. But no matter how desperate for food they are, you must prevent them from stealing even one beef. If they do, they shall never see home again."

"I myself will guard the herds of the Sun-Titan," said Ulysses, "and not one beef shall be taken. Thank you, wise Teiresias."

"Go now. Take your men aboard the ship and go. Sail up the black river toward the upper air."

"But now that I am here and have come such a long and weary way to get here, may I not see some of the famous sights? May I not see Orion hunting, Minos judging? May I not dance with the heroes in the Fields of Asphodel? May I not see Tantalus thirsting, or my own grandfather, Sisyphus, rolling his eternal stone up the hill?"

"No," said Teiresias. "It is better that you go. You have been here too long already, I fear; too long exposed to these bone-bleaching airs. You may already be tainted with death, you and your men, making your fates too heavy for any ship to hold. Embark then. Sail up the black river. Do not look back. Remember our advice and forget our reproaches, and do not return until you are properly dead."

Ulysses ordered his men aboard. He put down the helm. There was still no wind. But the sails stretched taut, and the ship pushed upriver. Heeding the last words of the old sage, he did not look back, but he heard the voice of his mother calling, "Good-bye . . . good-bye . . ." until it grew faint as his own breath.

The Wandering Rocks

THEY sailed out of darkness into light, and their hearts danced with joy to see blue water and blue sky again. A fair west wind plumped their sails and sped them toward home.

"If this wind keeps blowing," said Ulysses to himself, "perhaps we can skirt the dangerous islands they spoke of; sail right around these Sirens and these tide-drinking, man-eating monsters and find our way home without further mishap. True, it was foretold differently, but what of that? How reliable are such prophecies, after all? Ajax and Achilles were always better at fighting than thinking—why should they be wiser dead than alive? And Elpenor—my most inept hand? Must I take his word for what is going to happen? Why, that fall from the mast must have scattered the few wits he had. Besides, they were all ghosts down there, advising me, and ghosts are gloomy by nature, as everyone knows. They like to frighten people; it's the way they've been trained. No! By the gods, I will not accept all this evil as inevitable but will stretch my sails to the following wind and speed for Ithaca."

At that very moment he heard a strange sound, not a sound the wind makes, nor the water, nor the voice of man or gull. He looked about, searched sky and water. He saw nothing. Then he turned over the helm to one of the sailors and climbed the mast. There he could see for miles over the dancing water. And far to the south he saw tiny black things floating, so small he could not tell whether he was imagining them or not. But they grew larger even as he watched. And as they came near, the strange, moaning, grinding sound grew louder and louder.

"What are they?" he said to himself. "They look like rocks, but rocks don't float. Can they be dolphins? Not whales, surely—whales spout. And all fish are voiceless. What is it then that comes and cries upon the silence of the seas? Another evil spawned by the stubborn god who pursues me? But what?"

By now the objects were close enough to see, and he saw that they were indeed rocks. A floating reef of rocks. Jagged boulders bobbing on the waves like corks. Rubbing against each other and making that moaning, grinding sound. And coming fast, driving purposefully toward the ship.

"Port the helm!" roared Ulysses.

The ship swung northward as the rocks pressed from the south.

"Floating rocks," said Ulysses. "Who has seen their like? This is a wonder unreported by any traveler. We see a new thing today, and I should like to see the last of it. Are they following us? Are they driven by some intelligence? Or are we caught in a trick of tide that moves them so? I shall soon see."

He took the helm himself then and sailed the ship in a circle to give the rocks a chance to pass by. But to his horror he saw the rocks begin to circle also, keeping always between him and the open sea to the south. They held the same distance now. He sheared off northward; they followed, keeping the same distance. But when he turned and headed south, they held their place. He saw them loom before his bow, jagged and towering, ready to crush his hull like a walnut. And he had to swing off again and dart away northward, as the crew raised a shout of terror.

So he set his course north by northwest, thinking sadly: "I see that I can avoid nothing that was foretold. I cannot bear southward around the Isle of the Sun where lurk the demons and monsters I have been warned against but must speed toward them as swiftly as toward a rendezvous with loved ones. These rocks shepherd me; they herd this vessel as a stray sheep is herded by the shepherd's dog, driving me toward that which the vengeful gods have ordained. So be it then. If I cannot flee, then I must dare. Heroes are made, I see, when retreat is cut off. So be it."

He set his course for the Isle of the Sun-Titan, which men called Thrinacia, and which we know now as Sicily.

All through the night they sailed. In the darkness they lost sight of the rocks. But they could hear them clashing and moaning, keeping pace with the ship.

The Sirens

IN the first light of morning Ulysses awoke and called his crew about him.

"Men," he said. "Listen well, for your lives today hang upon what I am about to tell you. That large island to the west is Thrinacia, where we must make a landfall, for our provisions run low. But to get to the island we must pass through a narrow strait. And at the head of this strait is a rocky islet where dwell two sisters called Sirens, whose voices you must not hear. Now I shall guard you against their singing, which would lure you to shipwreck, but first you must bind me to the mast. Tie me tightly, as though I were a dangerous captive. And no matter how I struggle, no matter what signals I make to you, *do not release me*, lest I follow their voices to destruction, taking you with me."

Thereupon Ulysses took a large lump of the beeswax that was used by the sail mender to slick his heavy thread and kneaded it in his powerful hands until it became soft. Then he went to each man of the crew and plugged his ears with soft wax; he caulked their ears so tightly that they could hear nothing but the thin pulsing of their own blood.

Then he stood himself against the mast, and the men bound him about with rawhide, winding it tightly around his body, lashing him to the thick mast.

They had lowered the sail because ships cannot sail through a narrow strait unless there is a following wind, and now each man of the crew took his place at the great oars. The polished blades whipped the sea into a froth of white water and the ship nosed toward the strait.

Ulysses had left his own ears unplugged because he had to remain in command of the ship and had need of his hearing. Every sound means something upon the sea. But when they drew near the rocky islet and he heard the first faint strains of the Sirens' singing, then he wished he, too, had stopped his own ears with wax. All his strength suddenly surged toward the sound of those magical voices. The very hair of his head seemed to be tugging at his scalp, trying to fly away. His eyeballs started out of his head.

For in those voices were the sounds that men love:

Happy sounds like bird railing, sleet hailing, milk pailing. . . .

Sad sounds like rain leaking, tree creaking, wind seeking. . . .

Autumn sounds like leaf tapping, fire snapping, river lapping. . . .

Quiet sounds like snow flaking, spider waking, heart breaking. . . .

It seemed to him then that the sun was burning him to a cinder as he stood. And the voices of the Sirens purled in a cool crystal pool upon their rock past the blue-hot flatness of the sea and its lacings of white-hot spume. It seemed to him he could actually see their voices deepening into a silvery, cool pool and must plunge into that pool or die a flaming death.

He was filled with such a fury of desire that he swelled his mighty muscles, burst the rawhide bonds like thread, and dashed for the rail.

But he had warned two of his strongest men—Perimedes and Eurylochus—to guard him close. They seized him before he could plunge into the water. He swept them aside as if they had been children. But they had held him long enough to give the crew time to swarm about him. He was overpowered—crushed by their numbers—and dragged back to the mast. This time he was bound with the mighty hawser that held the anchor.

The men returned to their rowing seats, unable to hear the voices because of the wax corking their ears. The ship swung about and headed for the strait again.

Louder now, and clearer, the tormenting voices came to Ulysses. Again he was aflame with a fury of desire. But try as he might he could not break the thick anchor line. He strained against it until he bled, but the line held.

The men bent to their oars and rowed more swiftly, for they saw the mast bending like a tall tree in a heavy wind, and they feared that Ulysses, in his fury, might snap it off short and dive, mast and all, into the water to get at the Sirens.

Now they were passing the rock, and Ulysses could see the singers. There were two of them. They sat on a heap of white bones—the bones of shipwrecked sailors—and sang more beautifully than senses could bear. But their appearance did not match their voices, for they were shaped like birds, huge birds, larger than eagles. They had feathers instead of hair, and their hands and feet were claws. But their faces were the faces of young girls.

When Ulysses saw them he was able to forget the sweetness of their voices because their look was so fearsome. He closed his eyes against the terrible sight of these bird-women perched on their heap of bones. But when he closed his eyes and could not see their ugliness, then their voices maddened him once again, and he felt himself straining against the bloody ropes. He forced himself to open his eyes and look upon the monsters, so that the terror of their bodies would blot the beauty of their voices.

But the men, who could only see, not hear the Sirens, were so appalled by their aspect that they swept their oars faster and faster, and the black ship scuttled past the rock. The Sirens' voices sounded fainter and fainter and finally died away.

When Perimedes and Eurylochus saw their captain's face lose its madness, they unbound him, and he signaled to the men to unstop their ears. For now he heard the whistling gurgle of a whirlpool, and he knew that they were approaching the narrowest part of the strait, and must pass between Scylla and Charybdis.

Scylla and Charybdis

ULYSSES had been told in Tartarus of these two monsters that guard the narrow waterway leading to Thrinacia. Each of them hid beneath its own huge rock, which stood side by side and were separated only by the width of the strait at its narrowest point.

Charybdis dwelt in a cave beneath the left-hand rock. Once she had been a superbly beautiful naiad, daughter of Poseidon, and very loyal to her father in his endless feud with Zeus, Lord of Earth and Sky. She it was who rode the hungry tides after Poseidon had stirred up a storm and led them onto the beaches, gobbling up whole villages, submerging fields, drowning forests, claiming them for the sea. She won so much land for her father's kingdom that Zeus became enraged and changed her into a monster, a huge bladder of a creature whose face was all mouth and whose arms and legs were flippers. And he penned her in the cave beneath the rock, saying:

"Your hunger shall become thirst. As you once devoured land belonging to me, now you shall drink the tide thrice a day— swallow it and spit it forth again—and your name will be a curse to sailors forever."

And so it was. Thrice a day she burned with a terrible thirst and stuck her head out of the cave and drank down the sea, shrinking the waters to a shallow stream, and then spat the water out again in a tremendous torrent, making a whirlpool near her rock in which no ship could live.

This was Charybdis. As for Scylla, who lived under the right-hand rock, she, too, had once been a beautiful naiad. Poseidon himself spied her swimming one day and fell in love with her and so provoked the jealousy of his wife, Amphitrite, that she cried:

"I will make her the most hideous female that man or god ever fled from!"

Thereupon she changed Scylla into something that looked like a huge, fleshy spider with twelve legs and six heads. She also implanted in her an insatiable hunger, a wild greed for human flesh. When any ship came within reach of her long tentacles, she would sweep the deck of sailors and eat them.

Ulysses stood in the bow as the ship nosed slowly up the strait. The roaring of the waters grew louder and louder, and now he saw wild feathers of spume flying as Charybdis sucked down the tide and spat it back. He looked at the other rock. Scylla was not in sight. But he knew she was lurking underneath, ready to spring. He squinted, trying to measure distances. The only chance to come through unharmed, he saw, was to strike the middle way between the two rocks, just beyond the suction of the whirlpool, and just out of Scylla's reach. But to do this meant that the ship must not be allowed to swerve a foot from its exact course, for the middle way was no wider than the ship itself.

He took the helm and bade his men keep a perfectly regular stroke. Then, considering further, he turned the helm over to Eurylochus and put on his armor. Grasping sword and spear, he posted himself at the starboard rail.

"For," he said to himself, "there is no contending with the whirlpool. If we veer off our course it must be toward the other monster. I can fight any enemy I can see."

The men rowed very carefully, very skillfully. Eurylochus chanted the stroke, and the black ship cut through the waters of the strait, keeping exactly to the middle way.

They were passing between the rocks now. They watched in amazement as the water fell away to their left, showing a shuddering flash of sea bed and gasping fish, and then roared back again with such force that the water was beaten into white froth. They felt their ship tremble.

"Well done!" cried Ulysses. "A few more strokes and we are through. Keep the way—the middle way!"

But, when measuring distance, he had been unable to reckon upon one thing. The ship was being rowed, and the great sweep oars projected far beyond the width of the hull. And Scylla, lurking underwater, seized two of the oars and dragged the ship toward her.

Dumbfounded, Ulysses saw the polished shafts of the oars which had been dipping and flashing so regularly suddenly snap like twigs, and before he knew what was happening, the deck tilted violently. He was thrown against the rail and almost fell overboard.

He lay on the deck, scrambling for his sword. He saw tentacles arching over him; they were like the arms of an octopus, but ending in enormous human hands.

He found his sword, rose to his knees, and hacked at the tentacles. Too late. The hands had grasped six sailors, snatched them screaming through the air and into the sea.

Ulysses had no time for fear. He had to do a number of things immediately. He roared to the crew to keep the ship on course lest it be swept into the whirlpool. Then he seized an oar himself and rowed on the starboard side where the oars had been broken.

From where he sat he could see Scylla's rock, could see her squatting at the door of her cave. He saw her plainly, stuffing the men into her six bloody mouths. He heard the shrieks of his men as they felt themselves being eaten alive.

He did not have time to weep, for he had to keep his crew rowing and tell the helmsman how to steer past the whirlpool.

They passed through the strait into open water. Full ahead lay Thrinacia with its wooded hills and long white beaches, the Isle of the Sun-Titan, their next landfall.

The Cattle of the Sun

INSTEAD of landing on Thrinacia, as the crew expected, Ulysses dropped anchor and summoned his two underchiefs, Eurylochus and Perimedes, to take counsel. He said:

"You heard the warning of old Teiresias down in Tartarus. You heard him say that this island belongs to Hyperion, the Sun-Titan, who uses it as a grazing land for his flocks. The warning was most dire: Whosoever of our crew harms these cattle in any way will bring swift doom upon himself and will never see his home again."

"We all heard the warning," said Eurylochus, "and everyone will heed it."

"How can you be so sure?" said Ulysses. "If this voyage has taught you nothing else, it should have proved to you that there is nothing in the world so uncertain as man's intentions, especially his good ones. No, good sirs, what I propose is that we change our plans about landing here and seek another island, one where death does not pasture."

"It will never do," said Eurylochus. "The men are exhausted. There is a south wind blowing now, which means we would have to row. We simply do not have the strength to hold the oars."

"Our stores are exhausted, too," said Perimedes. "The food that Circe gave us is almost gone. The water kegs are empty. We must land here and let the men rest and lay in fresh provisions."

53

"Very well," said Ulysses. "If it must be, it must be. But I am holding you two directly responsible for the safety of the sun-cattle. Post guards at night, and kill any man who goes near these fatal herds."

Thereupon the anchor was raised, and the ship put into harbor. Ulysses did not moor the ship offshore, but had the men drag it up on the beach. He sent one party out in search of game, another to fill the water kegs, and a third to chop down pine trees. From the wood was pressed a fragrant black sap, which was boiled in a big iron pot. Then he had the men tar the ship from stem to stern, caulking each crack.

The hunting party returned, downhearted. There seemed to be no game on the island, they told Ulysses, only a few wild pigs, which they had shot, but no deer, no bear, no rabbits, no game birds. Just the pigs and great herds of golden cattle.

The water party returned triumphantly, barrels full.

The men were so weary that Ulysses stood guard himself that night. Wrapped in his cloak, naked sword across his knees, he sat hunched near the driftwood fire, brooding into the flames.

"I cannot let them rest here," he said to himself. "If game is so scarce, they will be tempted to take the cattle. For hungry men the only law is hunger. No, we must put out again tomorrow and try to find another island."

The next morning he routed out the men. They grumbled terribly but did not dare to disobey. However, they were not fated to embark. A strong south wind blew up, almost gale strength, blowing directly into the harbor. There was no sailing into the teeth of it, and it was much too strong to row against.

"Very well," said Ulysses, "scour the island for game again. We must wait until the wind drops."

He had thought it must blow itself out in a day or so, but it was not to be. For thirty days and thirty nights the south wind blew, and they could not leave the island. All the wild pigs had been killed. The men were desperately hungry. Ulysses used all his cunning to find food. He had the men fish in the sea, dig the beaches for shellfish and turtle eggs, search the woods for edible roots and berries. They tore the clinging limpets off rocks and shot gulls. A huge pot was kept boiling over the driftwood fire, and in it the men threw anything remotely edible—sea polyps, sea lilies, fish heads, sand crabs—vile broth. But most days they had nothing else. And they grew hungrier and hungrier.

For thirty days the strong south wind blew, keeping them beached. Finally, one night when Ulysses was asleep, Eurylochus secretly called the men together, and said, "Death comes to men in all sorts of ways. And however it comes, it is never welcome. But the worst of all deaths is to die of starvation. And to be forced to starve among herds of fat beef is a hellish torture that the gods reserve for the greatest criminals. So I say to you men that we must disregard the warning of that meddlesome ghost, Teiresias, and help ourselves to this cattle. We can do it now while Ulysses sleeps. And if indeed the Sun-Titan is angered and seeks vengeance—well, at least we shall have had one more feast before dying."

It was agreed. They went immediately into the meadow. Now, Hyperion's cattle were the finest ever seen on earth. They were enormous, sleek, broad-backed, with crooked golden horns, and hides of beautiful dappled gold and white. And when the men came among them with their axes, they were not afraid, for no one had ever offered them any harm. They looked at the men with their great plum-colored eyes, whisked their tails, and continued grazing.

The axes rose and fell. Six fine cows were slaughtered. Because they knew they were committing an offense against the gods, the men were very careful to offer sacrifice. Upon a makeshift altar they placed the fat thigh-bones and burned them as offerings. They had no wine to pour upon the blazing meat as a libation, so they used water instead, chanting prayers as they watched the meat burn.

But the smell of the roasting flesh overcame their piety. They leaped upon the carcasses like wild beasts, ripped them apart with their hands, stuck the flesh on spits, and plunged them into the open fire.

Ulysses awoke from a dream of food. He sniffed the air and realized it was no dream, that the smell of roasting meat was real. He lifted his face to the sky, and said, "O mighty ones, it was unkind to let me fall into sleep. For now my men have done what they have been told they must not do."

He drew his sword and rushed off to the light of the fire.

But just then Zeus was hearing a more powerful plea. For the Sun-Titan had been informed immediately by the quick spies that serve the gods, and now he was raging upon Olympus.

"O Father Zeus," he cried, "I demand vengeance upon the comrades of Ulysses who have slaughtered my golden kine. If they are spared, I will withdraw my chariot from the sky. No longer will I warm the treacherous earth but will go to Hades and shine among the dead."

"I hear you, cousin," said Zeus, "and promise vengeance."

Ulysses dashed among the feasting crew, ready to cut them down even as they squatted there, eating.

"Wait," cried Eurylochus. "Hold your hand. These are not the Sun-God's cattle, but seven stags we found on the other side of the island."

"Stags?" roared Ulysses. "What kind of monstrous lie is this? You know there are no stags on this island."

"They were there," said Eurylochus. "And now they are here. Perhaps the gods relented and sent them as food. Come, eat, dear friend, and do not invent misdeeds where none exist."

Ulysses allowed himself to be persuaded, sat down among the men, and began to eat with ravenous speed. But then a strange thing happened. The spitted carcasses turning over the fire began to low and moo as though they were alive; one of the flayed hides crawled over the sand to Ulysses, and he saw that it was dappled gold and white and knew he had been tricked.

Once again he seized his sword and rushed toward Eurylochus.

"Wait!" cried Eurylochus. "Do not blame me. We have not offended the gods by our trickery. For the south wind has fallen—see? The wind blows from the north now, and we can sail away. If the gods were angry, Ulysses, would they send us a fair wind?"

"To the ship!" shouted Ulysses. "We sail immediately."

The men gathered up the meat that was left and followed Ulysses to the beached ship. They put logs under it and rolled it down to the sea. Here they unfurled the sail and slid out of the harbor.

Night ran out and the fires of dawn burned in the sky. The men hurried about their tasks, delighted to be well fed and sailing again, after the starving month on Thrinacia.

But then Ulysses, observing the sky, saw a strange sight. The sun seemed to be frowning. He saw that black clouds had massed in front of it. He heard a rustling noise and looked off westward, where he saw the water ruffling darkly.

"Down sail!" he shouted. "Ship the mast!"

Too late. A wild west wind came hurtling across the water and pounced on the ship. There was no time to do anything. Both forestays snapped. The mast split and fell, laying its white sail like a shroud over the ship. A lightning bolt flared from the blue sky and struck amidships. Great billows of choking yellow smoke arose. The heat was unbearable. Ulysses saw his men diving off the deck, garments and hair ablaze and hissing like cinders when they hit the water.

He was still shouting commands, trying to chop the sail free and fighting against gale and fire. But he was all alone. Not one man was aboard. The ship fell apart beneath him. The ribs were torn from the keel. The ship was nothing but a mass of flaming timbers, and Ulysses swam among them. He held on to the mast, which had not burned. Pushing it before him, he swam out of the blazing wreckage. He found the keel floating free. The oxhide backstay was still tied to the head of the mast; with it he lashed mast and keel together into a kind of raft.

He looked about, trying to find someone to pull aboard. There was no one. He had no way of steering the raft but had to go where the wind blew him. And now, to his dismay, he found the wind shifting again. It blew from the south, which meant that he would be pushed back toward the terrible strait.

All day he drifted, and all night. When dawn came, it brought with it a roaring sucking sound, and he saw that he was being drawn between Scylla and Charybdis. He felt the raft being pulled toward the whirlpool. It was the very moment when Charybdis took her first drink of the day. She swallowed the tide and held it in her great bladder of a belly. The raft spun like a leaf in the outer eddies of the huge suction, and Ulysses knew that when he reached the vortex of the whirlpool, he and the raft would be drawn to the bottom and that he must drown.

He kept his footing on the raft until the very last moment, and just as it was pulled into the vortex, he leaped as high as he could upon the naked face of the rock, scrabbling for a hand-hold. He caught a clump of lichen, and clung with all his strength. He could climb no higher on the rock; it was too slippery for a foothold. All he could do was cling to the moss and pray that his strength would not give out. He was waiting for Charybdis to spit forth the tide again.

The long hours passed. His shoulders felt as though they were being torn apart by red-hot pincers. Finally he heard a great tumult of waters and saw it frothing out of the cave. The waves leaped toward his feet. And then he saw what he was waiting for—his raft came shooting up like a cork.

He dropped upon the timbers. Now he would have some hours of quiet water, he knew, before Charybdis drank again. So he kept to that side of the strait, holding as far from Scylla as he could, for he well remembered the terrible reach of her arms.

He passed safely beyond the rocks and out of the strait. For nine days he drifted under the burning sun, nine nights under the indifferent moon. With his knife he cut a long splinter from the timbers and shaped it into a lance for spearing fish. He did not get any. Then he lay on his back, pretending to be dead, and gulls came to peck out his eyes. He caught them and wrung their necks. He ate their flesh and drank their blood and so stayed alive.

On the tenth day he found himself approaching another island.

He was very weak. The island grew dim as he looked at it. A black mist hid the land, which was odd because the sun was shining. Then the sky tilted, and the black mist covered him.

Calypso

WHEN Ulysses awoke he found himself lying on a bed of sweet-smelling grass. The sun shone hotly, but he was in a pool of delicious cool shade under a poplar tree. He was still dizzy. The trees were swaying, and bright flowers danced upon the meadow. He closed his eyes, thinking, "I am dead then. The god that hunts me took pity and shortened my hard life, and I am now in the Elysian Fields."

A voice answered, "You have not died. You are not in the Elysian Fields. You have come home."

He opened his eyes again. A woman was bending over him. She was so tall that he knew she was no mortal woman but nymph or naiad or demigoddess. She was clad in a short tunic of yellow and purple. Her hair was yellow and long and thick.

"You are here with me," she said. "You have come home."

"Home? Is this Ithaca? Are you Penelope?"

"This is Ogygia, and I am Calypso."

He tried to sit up. He was too weak. "But Ithaca is my home," he said. "And Penelope is my wife."

"Home is where you dwell. And wives, I am told, often change. Especially for sailors. Especially for you. And now you belong to me, because this island and everything on it is mine."

Ulysses went back to sleep. For he believed he was dreaming and did not wish to wake up again and find himself on the raft. But when he awoke, he was still in his dream. He was strong enough now to sit up and look around. He was in a great grove hemmed by trees—alder and poplar and cypress. Across this meadow four streams ran, crossing each other, making a sound like soft laughter. The meadow was a carpet of wild flowers, violets, parsley, bluebells, daffodils, and cat-faced pansies. His bed had been made in front of a grotto, he saw. Over it a wild grapevine had been trained to fall like a curtain.

The vine curtain was pushed aside, and Calypso came out.

"You are awake," she cried, "and just in time for your wedding feast. The stag is roasted. The wine has been poured. No, don't move. You're still too weak. Let me help you, little husband."

She stooped and lifted him in her great white arms and carried him as easily as though he were a child in the grotto and set him before the hearth. A whole stag was spitted over the flame. The cave was carpeted with the skins of leopard and wolf and bear.

"Lovely and gracious goddess," said Ulysses, "tell me, please, how I came here. The last I remember I was on my raft, and then a blackness fell."

"I was watching for you," said Calypso. "I knew you would come, and I was waiting. Then your raft floated into sight. I saw you slump over and roll off the raft. And I changed you into a fish, for sharks live in this water and they are always hungry. As soon as I turned you into a fish, a gull stooped—and he would have had you—but I shot him with my arrow. Then I took my net and fished you out, restored you to your proper shape, fed you a broth of herbs, and let you sleep. That was your arrival, O man I have drawn from the sea. As for your departure, that will never be. Now eat your meat and drink your wine, for I like my husbands well fed."

Ulysses ate and drank and felt his strength return.

"After all," he thought, "things could be worse. In fact they have been much worse. This may turn out to be quite a pleasant interlude. She is certainly beautiful, this Calypso. Rather large for my taste and inclined to be bossy, I'm afraid. But who's perfect?"

He turned to her, smiling, and said, "You say you were waiting for me, watching for my raft. How did you know I would be coming?"

"I am one of the Titan brood," said Calypso. "Daughter of mighty Atlas, who stands upon the westward rim of the world bearing the sky upon his shoulders. We are the elder branch of the gods, we Titans. For us there is no before or after, only now, wherein all things are and always were and always will be. Time, you see, is a little arrangement man has made for himself to try to measure the immeasurable mystery of life. It does not really exist. So when we want to know anything that has happened in what you call 'before,' or what will happen in what you call 'after,' we simply shuffle the pictures and look at them."

"I don't think I understand."

"I have watched your whole voyage, Ulysses. All I have to do is poke the log in a certain way, and pictures form in the heart of the fire and burn there until I poke the log again. What would you like to see?"

"My wife, Penelope."

Calypso reached her long arm and poked the log. And in the heart of the flame Ulysses saw a woman, weaving.

"She looks older," he said.

"You have been away a long time. Only the immortals do not age. I was 2,300 years old yesterday. Look at me. Do you see any wrinkles?"

"Poor Penelope," said Ulysses.

"Don't pity her too much. She has plenty of company. She is presumed to be a widow, you know."

"Has she married again?"

"I weary of this picture. Would you like to see another?"

"My son, Telemachus."

She poked the fire again, and Ulysses saw the flickering image of a tall young man with red-gold hair. He held a spear in his hand and looked angry.

"How he has grown," murmured Ulysses. "He was a baby when I left. He is a young man now, and a fine one, is he not?"

"Looks like his father," said Calypso.

"He seems to be defying some enemy," said Ulysses. "What is happening?"

"He is trying to drive away his mother's suitors, who live in your castle now. She is quite popular—for an older woman. But then, of course, she has land and goods. A rich widow. You left her well provided, O sailor. She has many suitors and cannot decide among them. Or perhaps she enjoys their courtship too much to decide. But your son is very proud of his father, whom he does not remember, and seeks to drive the suitors from your castle."

"I had better go home and help him," said Ulysses.

"Put that out of your mind. It simply will not happen. Forget Ithaca, Ulysses. You are a hero, a mighty hero, and heroes have many homes, and the last is always the best. Look at this. See some of your exploits. Like many warriors, you were too busy fighting to know what really happened."

She poked the log again and again, and a stream of pictures flowed through the fire. Ulysses saw himself standing on a rock in the Cyclops' cave, holding the white-hot sword above the great sleeping eye, preparing to stab it in. He saw himself wrestling with the leather bag of winds that Aeolus had given him; saw himself running with the wolves and lions who had been Circe's lovers in the dark courtyard of her castle. Then, sword in hand, he saw himself hacking at Scylla's tentacles as she reached across the tilting deck for his men. Going back he saw himself before his homeward voyage crouched in the black belly of the wooden horse he had made. Next, climbing out of that horse after it had been dragged into the city and racing with lifted sword to slaughter the sleeping Trojan warriors. And, as he watched and saw the old battles refought, the men who had been his friends, and the monstrous enemies he had overcome, his heart sang with pride, and a drunken warmth stronger than the fumes of wine rose to his head, drowning out all the pictures of home.

He stood up and said, "Thank you for showing me myself, Calypso. I do seem to be a hero, don't I? And worthy to love a daughter of the Titans."

"Yes," said Calypso.

Now, Calypso had amused herself with shipwrecked sailors before. But she was hard to please, and none of them had lasted very long. When she was tired of someone she would throw him back into the sea. If she were feeling good-natured she would change him to gull or fish first. Indeed, the trees of the grove were filled with nesting sea birds—gull and heron and osprey and sand owls—who called to her at night, reproaching her.

"What is that clamor of birds?" said Ulysses.

"Just birds."

"Why do they shriek so?"

"They are angry at me for loving you. They were men once, like yourself."

"How did they get to be birds?"

"Oh, well, it's no very difficult transformation, when you know how. I thought they would be happier so."

"They don't sound very happy."

"They have jealous natures."

"You are not unlike Circe in some ways," said Ulysses. "You island goddesses are apt to be abrupt with your former friends. I've noticed this."

"It's a depressing topic, dear. Let's talk about me. Do you find me beautiful today?"

"More beautiful than yesterday, if that is possible. And no doubt will find you even lovelier tomorrow, since you have shown me the penalty of any inattention."

"Do not fear," said Calypso. "You are not like the others. You are bolder and have more imagination. You are a hero."

"Perhaps you could persuade your feathered friends to nest elsewhere? They make me nervous."

"Nothing easier. I shall simply tell them to depart. If they do not, I shall change them all to grasshoppers, all save one, who will eat the rest and then die of overeating."

"Truly, you are wise and powerful, and fair beyond all women, mortal or immortal."

She smiled. "You have such an apt way of putting things," she said.

So Ulysses made himself at home on the island and passed the time hunting game, fishing the sea, and reveling with the beautiful Calypso. He was happy. Thoughts of home grew dim. The nymph taught him how to poke the magic log upon her hearth so that it would cast up fire pictures. And he sat by the hour on the great hearth, reading the flickering tapestry of days gone by and days to come. But she had instructed the log never to show him scenes of Ithaca, for she wished him not to be reminded of his home in any way, lest he be tempted to depart. But Ulysses was as crafty as she was, and after he had poked the log many times, asking it to show him what was happening on his island, and the log had cast up pictures of other times, other places, he realized that Calypso had laid a magic veto upon scenes of home. And this, instead of making him forget, made him more eager than ever to know what was happening to Telemachus and Penelope.

One day he went into the wood, snared a sea crow, and asked, "Can you speak?"

"Yes," said the crow.

"Were you once a man?"

"Once . . . once . . . at the time of your grandfather, Sisyphus. I was a clever man, a spy. That's why Calypso changed me into a crow when she grew weary of me, for of all creatures we are the best for spying and prying and tattling."

"Then you're the bird for me," cried Ulysses. "Listen, I wish you to fly to Ithaca. Go to my castle and see what is happening. Then come back and tell me."

"Why should I? What will you give me?"

"Your life."

"My life? I already have that."

"But not for long. Because if you refuse to do as I ask, I shall wring your neck."

"Hmmm," said the crow. "There is merit in your argument. Very well. I shall be your spy. Only don't let Calypso know. She'll catch me and feed me to the cat before I can report to you. I have a notion she'd like you to forget Ithaca."

"Fly away, little bird," said Ulysses, "and do what you have to do. I'll take care of things here."

The next day, at dusk, as he was returning from the hunt, he heard the crow calling from the depth of an oak tree.

"Greetings," said Ulysses. "Have you done what I asked?"

"I have flown to Ithaca," said the crow. "A rough journey by sea, but not really so far as the crow flies. I flew to your castle and perched in an embrasure and watched and watched. Briefly, your son is grieving, your wife is weaving, and your guests are *not* leaving."

"What does my wife weave?"

"Your shroud."

"Has she decided so soon that I am dead? I have been gone scarcely twenty years."

"She is faithful. But the suitors, who are brawling, ill-mannered young men, are pressing her to choose one of them for a husband. However, she refuses to choose until she finishes the shroud. And it has been three years a-weaving, for each night she rips up the work she has done by day, so the shroud is never finished. But the suitors grow impatient. They are demanding that she finish her weaving and choose a groom. Your son opposes them. And they threaten to kill him unless he steps aside."

"Thank you, crow," said Ulysses.

"What will you do now—try to escape?"

"Escape? I do not consider myself a captive, good bird. I shall simply inform Calypso that I intend to leave and ask her to furnish transportation."

"You make it sound easy," said the crow. "Good luck."

And he flew away.

Ulysses went to Calypso in her grotto, fell on his knees before her, and said, "Fair and gracious friend, you have made me happier than any man has a right to be, especially an unlucky one. But now I must ask you one last great favor."

Calypso frowned. "I don't like the sound of that," she said. "What do you mean 'last'? Why should I not go on doing you favors?"

"I must go home."

"This is your home."

"No. My home is Ithaca. Penelope is my wife. Telemachus is my son. I have enemies. They live in my castle and steal my goods. They wish to kill my son and take my wife. I am a king. I cannot tolerate insults. I must go home."

"Suppose you do go home, what then?"

"I will contend with my enemies. I will kill them or they will kill me."

"You kill them, say—then what?"

"Then I live, I rule. I don't know. I cannot read the future."

"I can. Look."

She poked the magic log. Fire pictures flared. Ulysses saw himself sitting on his throne. He was an old man. Penelope was there. She was an old woman.

"You will grow old . . . old. . . ." Calypso's voice murmured in his ear, unraveling in its rough purring way like raw silk. "Old . . . old . . . You will live on memories. You will eat your heart out recalling old glories, old battles, old loves. Look . . . look into the fire."

"Is that me?"

"That's you, humping along in your old age among your hills, grown dry and cruel."

"What is that on my shoulder?"

"An oar."

"Why do I carry an oar where there is no sea?"

"If you go back to Ithaca, you will meet great trouble. You will be driven from your throne and be forced to carry an oar on your shoulder until you come to a place where no man salts his meat, and where they think the oar is a winnowing-fan. Then, if you abase yourself to Poseidon, he may forget his hatred for a while and grant you a few more years."

"Is that me standing at the shore?"

"That is you."

"Who is that young man?"

"Your son."

"Not Telemachus?"

"Another son. A fiercer one."

"Why does his spear look so strange?"

"It is tipped with the beak of a stingray."

"Why does he raise it against me?"

"To kill you, of course. And so death will come to you from the sea at the hands of your own son. For you angered the god of the sea by wounding his son, and he does not forgive."

She tapped the log and the fire died.

"Do you still want to go back to Ithaca?" she said.

"Will my future be different if I stay here?"

"Certainly. If you stay with me, it will be entirely different. You will no longer be a mortal man. I will make you my eternal consort, make you immortal. You will not die or grow old. This will be your home, not only this island, but wherever the Titans rule."

"Never die, never grow old. It seems impossible."

"You are a man to whom impossible things happen," said Calypso. "Haven't you learned that by now?"

"'*Never*' . . ." said Ulysses. "'*Always*' . . . These are words I find hard to accept."

"Do not think you will be bored. I am expert at variety. I deal in transformations, you know. I can change our forms at will. We can love each other as lion and lioness, fox and vixen. Touch high as eagles, twine as serpents, be stallion and mare. We can fly and prowl and swim. You can be a whale once and seek me deeply, or a tomcat, perhaps, weird voice burning the night, crying murder and amour. And then . . . then . . . we can return to this bowered island as Calypso and Ulysses, goddess and hero."

"You are eloquent," said Ulysses. "And you need no eloquence, for your beauty speaks more than any words. Still, I cannot be immortal, never to die, never to grow old. What use is courage then?"

Calypso smiled at him. "Enough discussion for one night. You have time to decide. Take five or ten years. We are in no hurry, you and I."

"Five or ten years may seem little to an immortal," said Ulysses. "But I am still a man. It is a long time for me."

"That's just what I said," said Calypso. "It is better to be immortal. But think it over."

The next morning, instead of hunting, Ulysses went to the other side of the island and built an altar of rocks and sacrificed to the gods. He poured a libation of unwatered wine, and raised his voice:

"O great gods upon Olympus—thunder-wielding Zeus and wise Athene, earth-shaking Poseidon, whom I have offended, golden Apollo—hear my prayer. For ten years I fought in Troy and for ten more years have wandered the sea, been hounded from island to island, battered by storms, swallowed by tides. My ships have been wrecked, my men killed. But you have granted me life. Now, I pray you, take back the gift. Let me join my men in Tartarus. For if I cannot return home, if I have to be kept here as a prisoner of Calypso while my kingdom is looted, my son slain, and my wife stolen, then I do not wish to live. Allow me to go home, or strike me dead on the spot."

His prayer was carried to Olympus. Athene heard it. She went to Zeus and asked him to call the gods into council. They met in the huge throne room. As it happened, Poseidon was absent. He had ridden a tidal wave into Africa, where he had never been, and was visiting the Ethiopians.

Athene said, "O father Zeus, O brother gods, I wish to speak on behalf of Ulysses, who of all the mighty warriors we sent to Troy has the most respect for our power and the most belief in our justice. Ten years after leaving the bloody beaches of Troy he has still not reached home. He is penned now on an island by Calypso, daughter of Atlas, who uses all her Titanic entice-ments to keep him prisoner. This man's plight challenges our Justice. Let us help him now."

Zeus said, "I do not care to be called unjust. I am forgetful sometimes, perhaps, but then I have much to think of, many af-fairs to manage. And remember, please, my daughter, that this man has been traveling the sea, which belongs to my brother Poseidon, whom he has offended. Poseidon holds a heavy grudge, as you know; he does not forgive injuries. Ulysses would have been home years ago if he had not chosen to blind Polyphemus, who happens to be Poseidon's son."

"He has paid for that eye over and over again," cried Athene. "Many times its worth, I vow. And the earth-shaker is not here, as it happens. He is off shaking the earth of Africa, which has been too dry and peaceable for his tastes. Let us take advantage of his absence and allow Ulysses to resume his voyage."

"Very well," said Zeus. "It shall be as you advise."

Thereupon he dispatched Hermes, the messenger god, to Ogygia. Hermes found Calypso on the beach singing a wild sea song, imitating now the voice of the wind, now the lisping, scraping sound of waves on a shallow shore, weaving in the cry of heron and gull and osprey, tide suck and drowned moons. Now, Hermes had invented pipe and lyre and loved music. When he heard Calypso singing her wild sea song, he stood upon the bright air, ankle wings whirring, entranced. He hov-ered there, listening to her sing. Dolphins were drawn by her voice. They stood in the surf and danced on their tails.

She finished her song. Hermes landed lightly beside her.

"A beautiful song," he said.

"A sad song."

"All beautiful songs are sad."

"Yes . . ."

"Why is that?"

"They are love songs. Women love men, and they go away. This is very sad."

"You know why I have come then?"

"Of course. What else would bring you here? The Olympians have looked down and seen me happy for a little while, and they have decreed that this must not be. They have sent you to take my love away."

"I am sorry, cousin. But it is fated that he find his way home."

"Fate . . . destiny . . . what are they but fancy words for the brutal decrees of Zeus. He cannot abide that goddesses should mate with mortal men. He is jealous, and that is the whole truth of it. He wants us all for himself. Don't deny it. When Eos, Goddess of Dawn, chose Orion for her lover, Zeus had his daughter, Artemis, slay him with her arrows. When Demeter, harvest wife, met Jasion in the plowed fields, Zeus himself flung his bolt, crippling him. It is always the same. He allowed Ulysses to be shipwrecked time and again. When I found him he was riding the timbers of his lost ship and was about to drown. So I took him here with me, cherished him, and offered to make him immortal. And now Zeus suddenly remembers, after twenty years, that he must go home immediately, because it is ordained."

"You can't fight Zeus," said Hermes gently. "Why try?"

"What do you want me to do?"

"Permit Ulysses to make himself a raft. See that he has provisions. Then let him depart."

"So be it."

"Do not despair, sweet cousin. You are too beautiful for sorrow. There will be other storms, other shipwrecks, other sailors."

"Never another like him."

"Who knows?"

He kissed her on the cheek and flew away.

Ino's Veil

IN her generous way, Calypso went beyond what the gods had ordered and provided Ulysses not with a raft but with a beautiful tight little vessel, sturdy enough for a long voyage, and small enough for one man to sail.

But he would have done just as well with a raft, for his bad luck held. He was seventeen days out of Ogygia, scudding along happily, when Poseidon, on his way back from Africa, happened to notice the little ship.

The sea god scowled and said:

"Can that be Ulysses? I thought I had drowned him long ago. One of my meddlesome relatives up there must be shielding him, and I have a good notion who. Well, I'll give my owlish niece a little work to do."

His scowl deepened, darkening the sun. He shook a storm out of his beard. The winds leaped, the water boiled. Ulysses felt the tiller being torn out of his hand. The boat spun like a chip. The sail ripped, the mast cracked, and Ulysses realized that his old enemy had found him again.

He clung to the splintered mast. Great waves broke over his head, and he swallowed the bitter water. He came up, gasping. The deck broke beneath him.

"Why am I fighting?" he thought, "Why don't I let myself drown?"

But he kept fighting by instinct. He pulled himself up onto a broken plank and clung there. Each boiling whitecap crested over him, and he was breathing more water than air. His arms grew too weak to hold the plank, and he knew that the next wave must surely take him under.

However, there was a Nereid near, named Ino, who hated Poseidon for an injury he had done her long before, and now she resolved to balk his vengeance. She swam to Ulysses' timber and climbed on.

He was snorting and gasping and coughing. Then he saw that he was sharing his plank with a green-haired woman wearing a green veil.

"Welcome, beautiful Nereid," he said. "Are you she who serves Poseidon, ushering drowned men to those caverns beneath the sea where the white bones roll?"

"No, unhappy man," she said, "I am Ino . . . and I am no servant of the windy widowmaker. I would like to do him an injury by helping you. Take this veil. It cannot sink even in the stormiest sea. Strip off your garments, wrap yourself in the veil, and swim toward those mountains. If you are bold and understand that you cannot drown, then you will be able to swim to the coast where you will be safe. After you land, fling the veil back into the sea, and it will find its way to me."

She unwound the green veil from her body and gave it to him. Then she dived into the sea.

"Can I believe her?" thought Ulysses. "Perhaps it's just a trick to make me leave the pitiful safety of this timber. Oh, well, if I must drown, let me do it boldly."

He pulled off his wet clothes and wrapped himself in the green veil and plunged into the sea.

It was very strange. When he had been on the raft, the water had seemed death-cold, heavy as iron, but now it seemed warm as a bath, and marvelously buoyant. He had been unable to knot the veil, but it clung closely to his body. When he began to swim he found himself slipping through the water like a fish.

"Forgive my suspicions, fair Ino," he cried. "Thank you . . . thank you . . ."

For two days he swam, protected by Ino's veil, and on the morning of the third day he reached the coast of Phaeacia. But he could not find a place to come ashore. For it was a rocky coast, and the water swirled savagely among jagged boulders. So he was in great trouble again. While the veil could keep him from drowning, it could not prevent him from being broken against the rocks.

The current caught him and swept him in. With a mighty effort he grasped the first rock with both hands and clung there, groaning, as the rushing water tried to sweep him on. But he clung to the rock like a sea polyp, and the wave passed. Then the powerful back-tow caught him and pulled him off the rock and out to sea. He had gained nothing. His arms and chest were bleeding where great patches of skin had been scraped off against the rock.

He realized that the only thing he could do was try to swim along the coast until he found an open beach. So he swam and he swam. The veil held him up, but he was dizzy from loss of blood. Nor had he eaten for two days. Finally, to his great joy, he saw a break in the reef. He swam toward it and saw that it was the mouth of a river. Exerting his last strength, he swam into the river, struggled against the current, swimming past the shore where the river flowed among trees. Then he had no more strength. He was exhausted.

He staggered ashore, unwrapped the veil from his body, and cast it upon the river so that it would be borne back to Ino. When he tried to enter the wood, he could not take another step. He collapsed among the reeds.

Nausicaa

IN those days, girls did not find their own husbands, especially princesses. Their marriages were arranged by their parents, and it all seemed to work out as well as any other way. But Nausicaa, sixteen-year-old daughter of the King and Queen of Phaeacia, was hard to please, and had been turning down suitors for two years now. Her father, Alcinous, and her mother,

Arete, were becoming impatient. There were several hot-tempered kings and princes who had made offers—for Nausicaa was very lovely—and Alcinous knew that if he kept turning them down he might find himself fighting several wars at once. He was a fine warrior and enjoyed leading his great fleet into battle. Still, he preferred his wars one at a time.

He told the queen that Nausicaa would have to be forced to choose.

"I was very difficult to please, too," said Arete. "But I think you'll admit I married well. Perhaps she, too, knows in her heart that if she bides her time the gods will send a mighty man to be her husband."

The king smiled. Arete always knew the right thing to say to him. So the discussion ended for that day. Nevertheless, the queen knew that her husband was right, and that the girl would have to choose.

That night Nausicaa was visited by a dream. It seemed to her that the goddess Athene stood over her bed, tall and gray-eyed, and spoke to her, saying, "How can you have a wedding when all your clothes are dirty? Take them to the river tomorrow and wash them."

The goddess faded slowly until all that was left was the picture on her shield—a snake-haired girl. And it seemed that the snakes writhed and hissed and tried to crawl off the shield to get at the dreamer. Nausicaa awoke, moaning. But she was a brave girl and went right back to sleep and tried to dream the same dream again, so that she could learn more about the wedding. But the goddess did not return.

The next morning she went to her mother and told her of the dream.

"I don't understand it," she said. "What wedding?"

"Yours, perhaps," said Arete.

"Mine? With whom?"

"The gods speak in riddles. You know that. Especially when they visit us in dreams. So you must do the one clear thing she told you. Take your serving girls to the river and wash your clothes. Perhaps, if you do that, the meaning will show itself."

Thereupon Nausicaa told her serving girls to gather all the laundry in the castle, and pile it in the mule cart. She also took food, a goatskin bottle of wine, and a golden flask of oil so that they could bathe in the river. Then they set off in the red cart, and the harness bells jingled as the mules trotted down the steep streets toward the river.

It was a sparkling morning. Nausicaa felt very happy as she drove the mules. They drove past the city walls, down the hill, and along a road that ran through a wood until they came to the river.

They dumped the clothes in the water and stamped on them, dancing and trampling and treading them clean. Then they dragged the clothes out, and pounded them on flat stones, afterwards spreading them to dry in the hot sun.

They then flung off their garments and swam in the river, scrubbing each other and anointing themselves with oil.

"Well, you look clean enough to get married," cried Nausicaa. "But it's easier to wash than to wed, isn't it, girls?"

The maidens giggled wildly, and Nausicaa shouted with laughter. She was so drunk with sun and water that she felt she could run up the mountain and dance all day and night. It was impossible to sit still. She seized a leather ball from the cart and flung it to one of her maids, who caught it and threw it back. Then the others joined in, and the girls frisked on the riverbank, tossing the ball back and forth.

Ulysses awoke from a deep sleep. He was still dazed and could barely remember how he had gotten among the reeds. He peered out, saw the girls playing, and then shrank back, for he did not wish to be seen as he was, naked and bruised.

But Nausicaa threw the ball so hard that it sailed over the heads of the girls and fell near the clump of reeds where Ulysses was hiding. A girl ran to pick it up, then shrank back, screaming.

"A man!" she cried. "A man—all bloody and muddy."

Ulysses reached out, plucked a spray of leaves from a fallen olive branch, and came out of the reeds.

The girls saw a naked man holding a club. His shoulders were bleeding, his legs muddy, and his hair crusted with salt. They fled, screaming. But Nausicaa stood where she was and waited for him.

"Is this why Athene sent me here?" she thought. "Is this my husband, come out of the river? Is this what I am to take after all the beautiful young men I have refused? Come back, you silly geese," she shouted to the girls. "Haven't you ever seen a man before?"

Then she turned to Ulysses, who had fallen to his knees before her.

"Speak, grimy stranger," she said. "Who are you, and what do you want?"

"Do not set your dogs upon me," said Ulysses. "I did not mean to surprise you in your glade."

"What talk is this? Are you out of your head?"

"Forgive me, but I know the fate of Actaeon, who came upon you in the wood. You turned him into a stag and had your hounds tear him to pieces."

"Whom do you take me for?"

"Why, you are Artemis, of course, Goddess of the Chase, maiden of the silver bow. I have heard poets praise your beauty, and I know you by your white arms. By your hair, and eyes, and the way you run—like light over water."

"Sorry to disappoint you, but I am not Artemis. I am Nausicaa. My father is king of this island. And I ask again—who are you?"

"An unlucky man."

"Where do you come from?"

"Strange places, princess. I am a sailor, hunted by a god who sends storms against me, wrecks my ships, kills my men. I come now from Ogygia, where I have been held captive by the Titaness, Calypso, who bound me with her spells. But as I was sailing away, a storm leaped out of the blue sky, smashing my boat. And I have been swimming in the sea for more than two days. I was dashed against the rocks of your coast but managed to swim around it till I found this river. When I came ashore here, I had no strength to go farther and fell where you found me."

"I suppose no one would look his best after spending two days in the sea and being beaten against rocks. You tell a good story, I'll say that for you. Why don't you bathe in the river now and try to make yourself look human again. We can give you oil for anointing, and clean garments belonging to my brother. Then you can follow me to the castle and tell your story there."

"Thank you, sweet princess," said Ulysses.

He took the flask of oil and went into the river and bathed and anointed himself. When he came out, he found clean garments waiting. The serving girls helped him dress and combed out his tangled hair.

"Well," said Nausicaa, "you look much improved. I can believe you're some kind of chieftain now. Are you married?"

"Yes."

"Of course. You would have to be, at your age."

"I have not seen my wife for twenty years. She considers herself a widow."

"Has she remarried?"

"Perhaps. I do not know. Last I heard, she was being besieged by suitors."

"I am besieged by suitors, too, but haven't found any I like well enough to marry."

As they spoke at the bank of the river, the serving girls had been piling the laundry into the mule cart.

"But I am thoughtless, keeping you here," said Nausicaa. "You need food and rest. You must come to the castle and finish your story there."

"The sight of your beauty is food and drink to me. And the sound of your voice makes me forget my weariness."

She laughed. "Are you courting me, stranger?"

"I am a homeless wanderer. I cannot court a princess. But I can praise her beauty."

"Come along to the castle. I want to introduce you to my father and mother. They are kind to strangers, very partial to brave men, and love to hear stories. And I want to hear more about you, too."

Now, that day, as it happened, King Alcinous had consulted an oracle, who prophesied, saying:

"I see danger. I see a mountain blocking your harbor, destroying your commerce. I sense the cold wrath of the god of the sea."

"But the earth-shaker has always favored us," said the king. "He has showered blessings upon this island. Our fleets roam far, return laden. Why should he be angered now?"

"I do not know. It is not clear, it is not clear. But I say to you, O King, beware of strangers, shipwrecks, storytellers. Believe no tale, make no loan, suffer no harm."

"I don't understand."

"Neither do I. But there is no need to understand, only to obey."

The oracle departed, leaving the king very thoughtful.

Just at this time, Nausicaa was leading Ulysses into the courtyard of the castle. She bade her maids take him to the guest house.

"Wait till I send for you," she said. "Food will be brought, and wine."

She raced to her mother's chamber.

"Oh, Mother, Mother," she cried. "I'm so glad I obeyed the dream and went to the river to wash our clothes. What do you think I found there? A man, hiding in the reeds, naked and wounded. I soon set him right and brought him here. Such an interesting man."

"Brought him here? Here to the castle? Paraded a naked beggar through the streets for the whole town to see? My dear child, haven't you given them enough to gossip about?"

"He's no beggar, Mother. He's a sailor or a pirate or something. Such stories he tells. Listen, he landed on an island once where men eat flowers that make them fall asleep and forget who they are. So they sleep all day and pick flowers all night and are very happy. This man's crew went ashore and ate the flowers and forgot who they were and didn't want to go back to the ship, just sleep. But he dragged them back anyway. I'd like to try those flowers, wouldn't you?"

"Who is this man? What's his name?"

"They came to another island where the sun and moon chase each other around the sky, and day flashes on like a lamp when you pass your hand over it. But you know who lived there? Giant cannibals, tall as trees, and they killed most of his men and cooked them in a big pot and broke two of his ships—and he had only one left."

"I asked you his name."

"I don't know. He didn't tell me. It's a secret or something."

"Do you believe everything he tells you?"

"Oh, yes. He's not exactly handsome, but very strong-looking, you know. Too old though, much too old. And married, of course. But I don't think he gets along with his wife. You can see he has suffered. You can see by his eyes."

"Where is he now?"

"In the guest house. Don't you think we should have a banquet for him tonight? He's a distinguished visitor, isn't he—all those things he did?"

"We don't quite know what he is, do we, dear? I think I had better meet him myself first. Your father's in a funny mood. Met with the oracle today, and something went wrong, I think."

"Yes, yes, I want you to meet him before Father does. I want to know what you think. Shall I fetch him?"

"I'll send a servant, child. You are not to see him again until I find out more about him. Do you understand?"

"Oh, yes, find out, find out! Tell me everything he says."

Queen Arete spoke with Ulysses, and then went to her husband, the king, and told him of their visitor. She was amazed to see his face grow black with rage.

"By the gods," he cried. "These are foul tidings you bring. Only today the oracle warned against strangers, shipwrecks, and storytellers. And now you tell me our daughter has picked up some nameless ruffian who combines all three—a shipwrecked stranger telling wild tales. Precisely what is needed to draw upon us the wrath of the sea god. I shall sacrifice him to Poseidon, and there will be an end to it."

"You may not do that," said Arete.

"Who says 'may not' to me? I am king."

"Exactly why you may not. Because you are king. The man comes to you as a supplicant. He is under your protection. If you harm him, you will bring down upon yourself the wrath of all the gods—not just one. That is the law of hospitality."

So the king ordered a great banquet that night to honor his guest. But certain young men of the court who were skilled at reading the king's moods knew that he was displeased and decided to advance themselves in his favor by killing the stranger and making it seem an accident.

"We will have games in the courtyard," said Euryalus, their leader. "We will hurl discus and javelin, shoot with the bow, wrestle, and challenge him to take part. And, when he does, it may be that some unlucky throw of javelin, or misshot arrow, will rid us of his company. Or, perchance, if he wrestles, he will find his neck being broken. It looks to be a thick neck, but he has been long at sea and is unused to such exercises."

So the young men began to hold their contests in the courtyard. When Ulysses stopped to watch them, Euryalus stepped forth and said, "There is good sport here, stranger, if you care to play."

"No, thank you," said Ulysses. "I'll just watch."

"Yes, of course," said Euryalus. "These games are somewhat dangerous. And one can see that you are a man of prudence. But then, of course, you are rather old for such sports, aren't you?"

He laughed sneeringly, picked up the heavy discus, whirled, and threw. It sailed through the air and landed with a clatter far away. All the young men laughed and cheered.

"Where I come from," said Ulysses, "such little discs are given babies to teethe on. The grown men need a bit more to test them."

He strode over to a battle chariot and broke off one of its wheels at the axle. It was a very heavy wheel, of oak bound with brass. He hefted it, and said:

"A little light, but it will do."

For he was filled with the wild rage that makes a man ten times stronger than he really is. He cradled the great wheel, whirled, and threw. It flew through the air, far past where the discus had landed, and thudded against the inner wall of the courtyard, knocking a hole in it. He turned to the others, who were paralyzed with amazement.

"Poor throw," he said. "But then, as you say, I'm rather old for such sport. However, since we are gathered here in this friendly fashion, let us play more games. If any of you would like to try me with sword or spear or dagger, or even a simple cudgel, let

him step forth. Or, perchance, there is one who would prefer to
wrestle?"

"That was well thrown, stranger," said Euryalus. "What is
your name?"

"I do not choose to tell you my name, O athlete."

"You are not courteous."

"If you care to teach me manners, young sir, I offer again.
Sword, spear, cudgel—any weapon you choose. Or no weapon at
all except our hands."

"We are civilized here in Phaeacia," said Euryalus. "We do not
fight with our guests. But I cannot understand why you refuse
to tell us your name."

"A god hunts me. If I say my name, it may attract his notice."

The young men nodded. For this is what was believed at that
time. But Euryalus ran to tell the king.

"I knew it," said Alcinous. "He carries a curse. He is the very
man the oracle warned me against. I must get rid of him. But the
law of hospitality forbids me to kill him under my roof. So tonight
we entertain him at a banquet. But tomorrow he leaves this castle,
and we shall find a way to see that he does not return."

"He is no weakling, this old sailor," said Euryalus. "He throws
the discus almost as well as I."

Now, all this time, Nausicaa had been thinking about the
stranger and weaving a plan, for she was determined to find out
who he was. She visited the old bard who had taught her to play
the lyre, and whose task it was to sing for the guests at the
royal feasts. She spoke and laughed with the old man and fed
him undiluted wine until he lost his wits. Then she locked him
in the stable, where he fell fast asleep on a bundle of straw, and
she departed with his lyre.

At the banquet that night, when the king called for the bard
to sing his tales, Nausicaa said, "The old man is ill and cannot
come. However, if you permit, I shall sing for your guests."

The king frowned. But Ulysses said, "This illness is a blessing, King. I think I should rather hear your black-haired daughter sing than the best bard who ever plucked a lyre."

The king nodded. Nausicaa smiled and began to sing. She
sang a tale of heroes. Of those who fought at Troy. She sang of
fierce Achilles and mighty Ajax. Of Menelaus and his shattering
war cry. Of brave Diomedes, who fought with Ares himself when
the war god came in his brazen chariot to help the Trojans.

She watched Ulysses narrowly as she sang. She saw his face
soften and his eyes grow dreamy, and she knew that he had

been there and that she was singing of his companions. But she still did not know his name.

Then she began to sing of that master of strategy, the great trickster, Ulysses. She sang of the wooden horse and how the warriors hid inside while the Trojans debated outside, deciding what to do. Some of them wanted to chop it to pieces; others wished to take it to a cliff and push it off; still others wanted to bring it within the city as an offering to the gods—which, of course, was what Ulysses wanted them to do. She told of the men hiding in the belly of the horse, listening to their fate being debated, and of the fierce joy that flamed in their hearts when they heard the Trojans decide to drag the horse within the walls. And of how, in the blackness of the night, they came out of the horse, and how Ulysses led the charge. She sang of him fighting there by the light of the burning houses, knee-deep in blood, and how he was invincible that night and carried everything before him.

And as she sang, she kept watching the stranger's face. She saw tears steal from between his clenched eyelids and roll down his cheeks. Amazed, the banqueters saw this hard-bitten sailor put his head in his hands and sob like a child.

He raised his streaming face and said, "Forgive me, gracious king. But the wonderful voice of your daughter has touched my heart. For you must know that I am none other than Ulysses, of whom she sings."

A great uproar broke out. The young men cheered. The women wept. The king said:

"My court is honored, Ulysses. Your deeds are known wherever men love courage. Now that I know who you are, I put all my power and goods at your disposal. Name any favor you wish, and it shall be yours."

Ulysses said: "O King, if I were the age I was twenty years ago when the ships were launched at Aulis, then the favor I would ask is your daughter's hand. For surely I have traveled the whole world over without seeing her like. I knew Helen, whose beauty kindled men to that terrible war. I knew the beauties of the Trojan court whom we took captive and shared among us. And, during my wanderings I have had close acquaintance with certain enchantresses whose charms are more than human, namely Circe and Calypso. Yet never have I seen a girl so lovely, so witty, so courteous and kind as your young daughter. Alas, it cannot be. I am too old. I have a wife I must return to, and a kingdom, and there are sore trials I must undergo before I can win again what belongs to me. So all I ask of you, great king, is

77

a ship to take me to Ithaca, where my wife waits, my enemies wait, my destiny waits."

Arete whispered to the king:

"Yes . . . yes . . . give him his ship tomorrow. I wish it could be tonight. See how your daughter looks at him; she is smitten to the heart. She is sick with love. Let him sail tomorrow. And be sure to keep watch at the wharf lest she stow away."

"It shall be as you say, mighty Ulysses," said the king. "Your ship will sail tomorrow."

So Ulysses departed the next day on a splendid ship manned by a picked crew, laden with rich goods the king had given him as hero gifts.

It is said that Athene drugged Poseidon's cup at the feast of the gods that night, so that he slept a heavy sleep and did not see that Ulysses was being borne to Ithaca. But Poseidon awoke in time to see the ship sailing back and understood what had happened. In a rage he snatched Athene's Gorgon-head shield, the sight of which turns men to stone, and flashed it before the ship just as it was coming into port after having left Ulysses at his island. The ship and all its crew turned to stone, blocking the harbor, as the oracle had foretold.

It is said, too, that Nausicaa never accepted any of the young men who came a-wooing, announcing that she was wedded to song. She became the first woman bard and traveled all the courts of the world singing her song of the heroes who fought at Troy, but especially of Ulysses and of his adventures among the terrible islands of the Middle Sea.

Some say that she finally came to the court of Ithaca to sing her song, and there she stayed. Others say that she fell in with a blind poet who took all her songs and wove them into one huge tapestry of song.

But it all happened too long ago to know the truth of it.

The Return

ULYSSES had landed on a lonely part of the shore. His enemies were in control of the island, and it was death to be seen. He stood on the empty beach and saw the Phaeacian ship depart. He was surrounded by wooden chests, leather bags, great bales—the treasure of gifts he had been given by Alcinous.

He looked about, at the beach and the cliff beyond, the wooded hills the color of the sky. He was home after twenty years, but it did not seem like home. It seemed as strange and unfriendly as any of the perilous isles he had landed on during his long wanderings. And he knew that Ithaca would not be his again until he could know it as king, until he had slain his enemies and regained his throne.

His first care was to find a cave in the cliffside, and there stow all his treasure. He moved swiftly now; he had planned his first moves on his homeward trip. It had helped him keep his thoughts away from Nausicaa. He took off his rich cloak and helmet and breastplate and hid them in the cave he had found, then laid his sword and spear beside them. He tore his tunic so that it hung in rags. He scooped up mud and smeared his face and arms and legs. Then he huddled his shoulders together and practiced a limping walk. Finally he was satisfied and began to hump away along the cliff road, no longer a splendid warrior, but a feeble old beggar.

He made his way to the hut of his swineherd, Eumaeus, a man his own age, who had served him all his life, and whom he trusted. Everything was the same here, he saw. The pigs were rooting in the trampled earth. There were four lanky hounds who started from their sleep and barked as he came near.

A man came out of the hut and silenced the dogs. Ulysses felt the tears well in his eyes. It was Eumaeus, but so old, so gray.

"What do you want?" said the swineherd.

"Food, good sir. Such scraps as you throw to the hogs. I am not proud, I am hungry."

"Are you a native of these parts?" said Eumaeus.

"No. I come from Crete."

"A long way for a beggar to come."

"I was not always a beggar. I was a sailor once . . . yes, and a captain of ships. I have seen better days."

"That's what all beggars say."

"Sometimes it's true. I once met a man from Ithaca, a mighty warrior and the most famous man I have ever met. He gave me a good opinion of Ithaca. It is a place, I know, where the hungry and helpless are not spurned."

"I suppose this man you met was named Ulysses."

"Why, yes. How did you guess?"

"Because I have heard that tale so many times. Do you think you're the first beggar to come slinking around, pretending to have news of our king? Everyone knows that he vanished on his journey home from Troy. Beggars swarm all over us trying to get some supper by telling lies."

"Then you will give me no food?"

"I didn't say that. Even liars have to eat. Ulysses never turned a beggar away, and neither will I."

The swineherd fed Ulysses and then let him rest by the fire. Ulysses pretended to sleep but watched his host through half-closed eyes and saw that the man was staring at him. He stretched and yawned.

"Are you sure you're a stranger to this island?" said Eumaeus. "Seems to me I've seen you before."

"No," said Ulysses. "You are mistaken. What shall I do now? Have I worn out my welcome, or may I sleep on your hearth tonight?"

"What will you do tomorrow?"

"Go to the castle and beg."

"You will not be welcome there."

"Why not? I will tell them how I met your king, and how kind he was to me. That should make them generous."

"It won't," said Eumaeus. "It will probably get you killed. Those who hold the castle now want to hear nothing about him—except the sure news of his death."

"How is that?"

"They hate him, because they do him harm. There are more than a hundred of them—rude, brawling young princes from neighboring islands and thievish young nobles of this island. They dwell in his castle as if they had taken it after a siege and seek to marry his wife, Penelope, refusing to leave until she accepts one of them. They drink his wine, devour his stores, break up the furniture for firewood, roister all night, and sleep all day. Do you know how many hogs I have to bring them? Fifty a day. That is how gluttonous they are. My herds are shrinking fast, but they say they will kill me the first day I fail to bring them fifty hogs."

"I heard he had a grown son. Why does he not defend his father's goods?"

"He's helpless. There are too many of them."

"Is he at the castle now?"

"No one knows where he is. He slipped away one night. Just as well. They were planning to kill him. The rumor is that he took ship and crew and went to seek his father. I hope he stays away. They will surely kill him if he returns."

"I go there tomorrow," said Ulysses. "It sounds like splendid begging. Such fiery young men are frequently generous, especially with other people's goods."

"You don't know them," said Eumaeus. "They are like wild beasts. But you cannot keep a fool from his folly. Go, if you must. In the meantime, sleep."

Now, upon this night Telemachus was at sea, sailing toward Ithaca. He had found no news of his father and was coming home with a very heavy heart. He would have been even more distressed had he known that a party of the wicked suitors were lying in wait for him aboard a swift ship full of fighting men. The ship was hidden in a cove, and the suitors meant to pounce upon him as he put into port.

But Athene saw this and made a plan. She went to Poseidon and said:

"I know you are angry with me, Uncle, for helping Ulysses. But now I wish to make it up to you. See, down there is a ship from Ithaca." She pointed to the suitors' vessel. "No doubt it holds friends of Ulysses, sailing out to meet their king. Why not do them a mischief?"

"Why not?" growled Poseidon.

And he wound a thick black mist about the suitors' ship so that it was impossible for the helmsman to see.

"Nevertheless," he said to Athene. "I still owe Ulysses himself a great mischief. I have not forgotten. In the meantime, let his friends suffer a bit."

The suitors' ship lay helpless in the mist, and Telemachus, sailing past them, ignorant of danger, put into port and disembarked.

Athene then changed herself into a young swineherd and hailed Telemachus on the beach:

"Greetings, my lord. I am sent by your servant, Eumaeus, to beg you to come to his hut before you go to the castle. He has important news to tell."

The lad set off, and Telemachus followed him toward the swineherd's hut.

Ulysses, dozing by the fire, heard a wild clamor of hounds outside, then a ringing young voice calling to them. He listened while the snarls turned to yaps of pleasure.

"It is my young master," cried Eumaeus, springing up. "Glory to the gods—he has come softly home."

Telemachus strode in. He was flushed from his walk. His face and arms were wet with the night fog, and his red-gold hair was webbed with tiny drops. To Ulysses he looked all aglitter, fledged by firelight, a golden lad. And Ulysses felt a shaft of wild joy pierce him like a spear, and for the first time he realized that he had come home.

But Telemachus was displeased to see the old beggar by the fire, for he wished to speak to Eumaeus privately to ask him how matters stood at the castle and whether it was safe for him to return.

"I do not wish to be discourteous, old man," he said, "but would you mind very much sleeping in the pig byre? You can keep quite warm there, and there are secret matters I wish to discuss."

"Be not wroth, my lord, that I have given this man hospitality," said Eumaeus. "He claims to have met your father once. A pitiful beggar's tale, no doubt, but it earned him a meal and a bed."

"Met my father? Where? When? Speak!"

But at the word "father," Ulysses could not endure it any longer. The voice of the young man saying that word destroyed all his strategies. The amazed Eumaeus saw the old beggar leap from his stool, lose his feebleness, grow wilder, taller, and open his arms and draw the young man to him in a great bear-hug.

"Dearest son," said the stranger, his voice broken with tears. "I am your father, Ulysses."

Telemachus thought he was being attacked and tensed his muscles, ready to battle for his life. But when he heard these words and felt the old man's tears burning against his face, then his marrow melted, and he laid his head on his father's shoulder and wept.

Nor could the honest old swineherd say anything; his throat was choked with tears, too. Ulysses went to Eumaeus and embraced him, saying: "Faithful old friend, you have served me well. And if tomorrow brings victory, you will be well rewarded."

Then he turned to his son and said, "The goddess herself must have led you here tonight. Now I can complete my plan. Tomorrow we strike our enemies."

"Tomorrow? Two men against a hundred? These are heavy odds, even for Ulysses."

"Not two men—four. There is Eumaeus here, who wields a good cudgel. There is the neatherd whom we can count on. And, no doubt, at the castle itself we will find a few more faithful servants. But it is not a question of numbers. We shall have surprise on our side. They think I am dead, remember, and that you are helpless. Now, this is the plan. You must go there in the morning, Telemachus, pretending great woe. Tell them you have learned on your journey that I am indeed dead and that now you must advise your mother to take one of them in marriage. This will keep them from attacking you—for a while anyway—

and will give us the time we need. I shall come at dusk, just before the feasting begins."

"What of my mother? Shall I tell her that you are alive?"

"By no means."

"It is cruel not to."

"It will prove a kindness later. Women cannot keep secrets, and we have a battle to fight. No, bid her dress in her finest garments, and anoint herself, and be as pleasant as she can to the suitors, for this will help disarm them. Understand?"

"I understand."

"Now, mark this well. You will see me being insulted, humiliated, beaten perhaps. Do not lose your temper and be drawn into a quarrel before we are ready to fight. For I must provoke the suitors to test their mettle and see where we should strike first."

Telemachus knelt in the firelight and said, "Sire, I shall do as you bid. I don't see how we can overcome a hundred strong men, but to die fighting at your side will be a greater glory than anything a long life can bestow. Thank you, Father, for giving me this chance to share your fortune."

"You are my true son," said Ulysses, embracing the boy tenderly. "The words you have just spoken make up for the twenty years of you I have missed."

Eumaeus banked the fire, and they all lay down to sleep.

Ulysses came to the castle at dusk the next day and followed Eumaeus into the great banquet hall, which was thronged with suitors. He humped along behind the swineherd, huddling his shoulders and limping. The first thing he saw was a dog lying near a bench. By its curious golden brown color he recognized it as his own favorite hunting hound, Argo. It was twenty-one years old, incredibly old for a dog, and it was crippled and blind and full of fleas. But Telemachus had not allowed it to be killed because it had been his father's.

As Ulysses approached, the dog's raw stump of a tail began to thump joyously upon the floor. The tattered old ears raised. The hound staggered to his feet, let out one wild bark of welcome, and leaped toward the beggar. Ulysses caught him in his arms. The dog licked his face, shivered, and died. Ulysses stood there holding the dead dog.

Then Antinous, one of the most arrogant of the suitors, who fancied himself a great jokster, strode up and said, "What are you going to do with that dead dog, man, eat him? Things aren't that bad. We have a few scraps to spare, even for a scurvy old wretch like you."

Ulysses said, "Thank you, master. I am grateful for your courtesy. I come from Crete, and—"

"Shut up!" said Antinous. "Don't tell me any sad stories. Now take that thing out and bury it."

"Yes, gracious sir. And I hope I have the honor of performing a like service for you one day."

"Oho," cried Antinous. "The churl has a tongue in his head. Well, well . . ."

He seized a footstool and smashed it over Ulysses' back. Telemachus sprang forward, blazing with anger, but Eumaeus caught his arm.

"No," he whispered. "Hold your peace."

Ulysses bowed to Antinous and said, "Forgive me, master. I meant but a jest. I go to bury the dog."

As soon as he left the room, they forgot all about him. They were agog with excitement about the news told by Telemachus, that Ulysses' death had been confirmed, and that Penelope would now choose one of them to wed. They crowded about Telemachus, shouting questions.

He said, "Gently, friends, gently. My mother will announce her choice during the course of the night. But first she desires that you feast and make merry."

The young men raised a great shout of joy, and the feasting began. Ulysses returned and went the round of the suitors, begging scraps of food. Finally he squatted near Eurymachus, a fierce young fellow whom he recognized to be their leader. Eurymachus scowled at him, but said nothing.

Into the banquet hall strode another beggar—a giant, shaggy man. He was a former smith who had decided that it was easier to beg than to work at the forge. He was well liked by the suitors because he wheedled and flattered them and ran their errands. He swaggered over to Ulysses and grasped him by the throat.

"Get out of here, you miserable cur," he said. "Any begging around here to do, I'll do it. I, Iros."

He raised his huge, meaty fist and slammed it down toward Ulysses' head. But Ulysses, without thinking, butted the man in the stomach, knocking him back against the wall.

"Look at that," cried Eurymachus. "The old souse has a head like a goat. For shame, Iros, you ought to be able to squash him with your thumb."

"Exactly what I intend to do," said Iros, advancing on Ulysses.

"A fight! A fight!" cried the suitors. "A beggar-bout. Good sport."

They crowded around the beggars, leaving just space enough for them to move.

Ulysses thought quickly. He could not risk revealing himself for what he was, yet he had to get rid of the fellow. So he shrank into his rags, as though fearful, allowing Iros to approach. Then, as the great hands were reaching for him and the suitors were cheering and jeering, he swung his right arm, trying to measure the force of the blow exactly. His fist landed on the smith's chin. The suitors heard a dry, cracking sound, as when you snap a chicken bone between your fingers, and they knew that their man's jaw was broken. He fell to the floor, unconscious, blood streaming from mouth and nose. Ulysses stooped and hoisted him over his shoulder and marched out of the banquet room, saying, "I'd better let him bleed outside. It will be less unpleasant for you gentlemen."

He draped the big man over a stile and came back.

"Well-struck, old bones," said Eurymachus. "You fight well for a beggar."

"A beggar?" said Ulysses. "What is a beggar, after all? One who asks for what he has not earned, who eats others' food, uses their goods? Is this not true? If so, young sir, I think you could become a member of our guild tomorrow."

Eurymachus carefully wiped the knife that he had been using to cut his meat and held the point to Ulysses' throat.

"Your victory over that other piece of vermin seems to have given you big ideas," he said. "Let me warn you, old fool, if you say one word more to me that I find unfitting, I will cut you up into little pieces and feed you to the dogs. Do you understand?"

"I understand, master," said Ulysses. "I meant but a jest."

"The next jest will be your last," growled Eurymachus.

Telemachus stepped between them and said, "Beggar, come with me to my mother. She has heard that you are a voyager and would question you about the places you have seen."

"What?" cried Eurymachus. "Take this stinking bundle of rags to your mother? She will have to burn incense for hours to remove the stench."

"You forget yourself, sir," said Telemachus. "You have not yet been accepted by my mother. She is still free to choose her own company."

Eurymachus played with his knife, glaring at Telemachus. He was angry enough to kill, but he did not wish to lose his chance with Penelope by stabbing her son. So he stepped aside and let Telemachus lead the old beggar out of the hall.

"You have done well," whispered Ulysses. "Another second and I would have been at the cur's throat, and we would have been fighting before we were ready. Besides, it is time I spoke to your mother. She enters our plans now."

When he was alone with Penelope, he sat with his face lowered. He did not wish to look at her. For her presence set up a great, shuddering tenderness inside him, and he knew that he had to keep himself hard and cruel for the work that lay ahead.

"In this chamber, you are not a beggar, you are a guest," said Penelope. "So take your comfort, please. Be at ease here with me, and tell me your tidings. I understand you met my husband, Ulysses, once upon your voyages."

"Beautiful queen," said Ulysses. "I knew him well. Better than I have admitted. I am a Cretan. I was a soldier. When the war with Troy started I went as part of a free-booting band to sell our swords to the highest bidder. We took service with your husband, Ulysses, and I fought under his banner for many years. Now his deeds before Troy have become famous in the time that has passed since the city was destroyed. Bards sing them from court to court all over the lands of the Middle Sea. Let me tell you a little story, though, that has never been told.

"I lay with him in that famous wooden horse, you know. We crouched in the belly of the horse that was dragged into Troy and set before the altar as an offering to the gods. The Trojans were crowding around, looking at this marvelous wooden beast, wondering at it, for such a thing had never been seen. But Queen Helen knew the truth somehow and, being a mischief-loving lady always, tapped on the belly of the horse, imitating the voices of the heroes' wives. She did it so cunningly that they could have sworn they heard their own wives calling to them and were about to leap out of the horse too soon, which would have been death.

"Now, Helen saved your voice till last. And when she imitated it, I heard Ulysses groan, felt him tremble. He alone was clever enough to know it was a trick, but your voice, even mimicked, struck him to the heart. And he had to mask his distress and use all his force and authority to keep the others quiet. A tiny incident, madame, but it showed me how much he loved you."

Penelope said: "Truly, this is a story never told. And yet I think that of all the mighty deeds that are sung, I like this little one best."

Her face was wet with tears. She took a bracelet from her wrist and threw it to him, saying, "Here is a gift. Small payment for such a tale."

"Thank you, Queen," said Ulysses. "My path crossed your husband's once again. My ship sailed past the Island of the Dawn. We had run out of water and were suffering from thirst, and there we saw a marvelous thing: A fountain of water springing out of the sea, pluming, and curling upon itself. We tasted it, and it was fresh, and we filled our water barrels. When I told about this in the next port, I learned how such a wonder had come to be. The enchantress, Circe, most beautiful of the daughters of the gods, had loved your husband and sought to keep him with her. But he told her that he must return to his wife, Penelope. After he left, she wept such tears of love as burned the salt out of the sea and turned it into a fountain of pure water."

Penelope took a necklace from her neck and said, "I liked the first story better, but this is lovely, too."

Ulysses said, "Thank you, Queen. I have one thing more to tell. Your husband and I were talking one time around the watch-fire on a night between battles, and he spoke, as soldiers speak, of home. He said that by the odds of war, he would probably leave you a widow. And, since you were beautiful, you would have many suitors and would be hard put to decide. Then he said, 'I wish I could send her this advice: Let her take a man who can bend my bow. For that man alone will be strong enough to serve her as husband, and Ithaca as king.'"

"Did he say that—truly?"

"Truly."

"How can I ask them to try the bow? They will jeer at me. They may feel offended and do terrible things."

"Disguise your intention. Tell them you cannot decide among such handsome, charming suitors. And so you will let their own skill decide. They are to hold an archery contest, using the great bow of Ulysses, and he who shoots best to the mark will win you as wife. They cannot refuse such a challenge, their pride will not permit them to. Now, good night, lady. Thank you for your sweet company. I shall see you, perchance, when the bow is bent."

"Good night, old wanderer," said Penelope. "I shall never forget the comfort you have brought me."

As Ulysses was making his way through the dark hallway, something clutched his arm and hissed at him:

"Ulysses . . . Ulysses . . . My master, my king . . . my baby . . . my lord . . ."

He bent his head and saw that it was an old woman and recognized his nurse, Eurycleia, who had known him from the day he was born, and who had tended him through his childhood.

"Dear little king," she wept. "You're back . . . you're back. I knew you would come. I told them you would."

Very gently he put his hand over her mouth and whispered: "Silence . . . No one must know, not even the queen. They will kill me if they find out. Silence . . . silence . . ."

She nodded quickly, smiling with her sunken mouth, and shuffled away.

Ulysses lurked outside the banquet hall until he heard a great roar from the suitors and knew that Penelope had come among them. He listened outside and heard her announce that she would choose the man, who, using her husband's great bow, would shoot best to the mark. He heard young men break into wild cheers. Then he hid himself as Telemachus, leading the suitors into the courtyard, began to set out torches for the shooting. Then it was that he slipped unnoticed into the castle and went to the armory where the weapons were kept. He put on a breastplate and arranged his rags over it so that he looked as he had before. Then he went out into the courtyard.

All was ready for the contest. An avenue of torches burned, making it bright as day. In the path of light stood a row of battle-axes driven into the earth, their rings aligned. Each archer would attempt to shoot through those rings. Until now only Ulysses himself had been able to send an arrow through all twelve axe-rings.

Now Penelope, followed by her servants, came down the stone steps carrying the great bow. She handed it to Telemachus, saying:

"You, son, will see that the rules are observed." Then, standing tall and beautiful in the torchlight, she said, "I have given my word to choose as husband he who best shoots to the mark, using this bow. I shall retire to my chamber now, as is fitting, and my son will bring me the name of my next husband. Now may the gods reward you according to your deserts."

She turned and went back into the castle. The noise fell. The young men grew very serious as they examined the great bow. It was larger than any they had ever seen, made of dark polished wood, stiffened by rhinoceros horn, and bound at the tips by golden wire. Its arrows were held in a bull-hide quiver; their shafts were of polished ash, their heads of copper, and they were tailed with hawk feathers.

Ulysses squatted in the shadows and watched the suitors as they crowded around Telemachus, who was speaking.

"Who goes first? Will you try, sir?"

Telemachus handed the bow to a prince of Samos, a tall, brawny man, and a skilled archer. He grasped the bow in his left hand, the dangling cord in his right, and tugged at the cord in the swift, sure movement that is used to string a bow. But it did not bend. He could not make the cord reach from one end to the other. He put one end of the bow on the ground and grasped the other end and put forth all his strength. His back muscles glistened like oil in the torchlight. The bow bent a bit under the enormous pressure, and a low sighing sound came from the crowd, but when he tugged on the cord, the bow twisted in his hand as if it were a serpent and leaped free. He staggered and almost fell. An uneasy laugh arose. He looked wildly about, then stomped away, weeping with rage.

Telemachus picked up the bow and said, "Next."

One by one they came; one by one they fell back. Not one of them could bend the bow. Finally, all had tried but Antinous and Eurymachus. Now Antinous was holding the bow. He shook his head and said:

"It is too stiff; it cannot be bent. It has not been used for twenty years. It must be rubbed with tallow and set by the fire to soften."

"Very well," said Telemachus.

He bade a servant rub the bow with tallow and set it near the fire. Ulysses kept out of sight. As they were waiting, Telemachus had a serving girl pass out horns of wine to the suitors. The men drank thirstily, but there was no laughter. They were sullen. Their hearts were ashen with hatred; they did not believe the bow could be softened. And Ulysses heard them muttering to each other that the whole thing was a trick.

Finally, Antinous called for the bow. He tried to string it. He could not.

"It cannot be done," he cried.

"No," said Eurymachus. "It cannot be done. I will not even try. This is a trick, another miserable, deceitful trick. Shroud that is never woven, bow that cannot be bent, there is no end to this widow's cunning. I tell you she is making fools of us. She will not be taken unless she be taken by force."

A great shouting and clamor arose. The suitors pressed close about Telemachus, hemming him in so tightly he could not draw his sword.

"Stop!" shouted Ulysses.

He cried it with all his force, in the great bellowing, clanging battle voice that had rung over spear shock and clash of sword to reach the ears of his men on so many fields before Troy. His great shout quelled the clamor. The amazed suitors turned to see the old beggar stride out of the shadows into the torchlight. He came among them, grasped the bow, and said, "I pray you, sirs, let me try."

Antinous howled like a wolf and sprang toward Ulysses with drawn sword. But Telemachus stepped between them and shoved Antinous back.

"My mother watches from her chamber window," he said. "Shall she see you as cowards, afraid to let an old beggar try what you cannot do? Do you think she would take any of you then?"

"Yes, let him try," said Eurymachus. "Let the cur have one last moment in which he pretends to be a man. And when he fails, as fail he must, then we'll chop his arms off at the shoulders so that he will never again be tempted to draw bow with his betters."

"Stand back," cried Telemachus. "Let him try."

The suitors fell back, their swords still drawn. Ulysses held the bow. He turned it lightly in his hands, delicately, tenderly, like a bard tuning his lyre. Then he took the cord and strung the bow with a quick turn of his wrist, and as the suitors watched, astounded, he held the bow from him and plucked the cord, making a deep vibrating harp note. Dumbfounded, they saw him reach into the quiver, draw forth an arrow, notch it, then bend the bow easily, powerfully, until the arrowhead rested in the circle of his fingers, just clearing the polished curve of the bow.

He stood there for a second narrowing his eyes at the mark, then let the arrow fly. The cord twanged, the arrow sang through the air, and passed through the axe-rings, all twelve of them.

Then, paralyzed by amazement, they saw him calmly sling the quiver over his shoulder and straighten up so that his breast-plate gleamed through the rags. He stood tall and, throwing back his head, spoke to the heavens:

"So the dread ordeal ends, and I come to claim my own. Apollo, dear lord of the silver bow, archer-god, help me now to hit a mark no man has hit before."

"It is he!" cried Antinous. "Ulysses!"

He died, shouting. For Ulysses had notched another arrow, and this one caught Antinous full in the throat. He fell, spouting blood.

No suitor moved. They looked at the twitching body that had been Antinous and felt a heavy sick fear, as if Apollo himself had come to loose his silver shaft among them.

Eurymachus found his tongue and cried:

"Pardon us, great Ulysses. We could not know you had returned. If we have done you evil, we will repay you, but hold your hand."

"Too late," said Ulysses. "Your evil can be repaid only by death. Now fight, or flee."

Then Eurymachus raised his sword and called to the suitors, "Up, men! Rouse yourselves, or he will kill us all as we stand here. Let us kill him first."

And he rushed toward Ulysses and fell immediately with an arrow through his chest. But he had roused them out of their torpor. They knew now that they must fight for their lives, and they charged across the yard toward Ulysses in a great half-circle.

Ulysses retreated slowly, filling the air with arrows, dropping a suitor with each shaft. But still they kept coming through the heaped dead. Now he darted backward suddenly, followed by Telemachus and Eumaeus, the swineherd, who had been protecting him with their shields. They ran into the dining hall and slammed the great portal, which immediately began to shake under the axe blows of the suitors.

"Overturn the benches," cried Ulysses. "Make a barricade."

The neatherd had joined them. And now Telemachus and the two men overturned the heavy wooden benches, making a barricade. They stood behind the wall of benches and watched the huge door splintering.

It fell. The suitors poured through. Now Ulysses shot the rest of his arrows so quickly that the dead bodies piled up in the doorway making a wall of flesh through which the suitors had to push their way.

His quiver was empty. Ulysses cast the bow aside and took two javelins. But he did not throw. For the suitors were still too far away, and he had to be sure of killing each time he threw.

A suitor named Agelaus had taken charge now, and he motioned to his men: "Let fly your spears—first you, then you, then the rest. And after each cast of spears let us move closer to the benches."

The long spears hurtled past the rampart. One grazed Telemachus' shoulder, drawing blood. And Ulysses, seeing the blood of his son, lost the battle-coldness for which he was famous among warriors. For the first time he felt the wild, hot, curdling rage rising in him like wine, casting a mist of blood before his eyes. Without making a decision to move, he felt his legs carrying him toward the great hearth. There he knelt and grasped the ring of the firestone—a huge slab of rock, large enough for a roasting ox. The suitors, charging toward the wall of benches, saw him rise like a vision out of the past, like some Titan in the War of the Gods, holding an enormous slab of rock over his head.

They saw their danger and tried to draw back, tried to scatter. But Ulysses had hurled the slab. It fell among the suitors and crushed them like beetles in their frail armor.

Only four of the suitors were left alive. Now Ulysses and Telemachus and the two servants were upon them—one to each and each killed his man. Then Ulysses and Telemachus raised a wild, exultant yell. Dappled with blood, they turned to each other, and Ulysses embraced his son.

"Well struck," he said. Then, to Eumaeus, "Thank you, good friend. Now go tell your queen, Penelope, that the contest has been decided, and the winner claims her hand."

"Father," said Telemachus. "When I reach my full strength, shall I be able to bend the great bow?"

"Yes," said Ulysses. "I promise you. I will teach you everything you have to know. I have come home."

Connected
Readings

Wanderlust

Gerald Gould

Beyond the East the sunrise, beyond the West the sea,
And East and West the wanderlust that will not let me be;
It works in me like madness, dear, to bid me say good-by!
For the seas call and the stars call, and oh, the call of the sky!

I know not where the white road runs, nor what the blue
    hills are,
But man can have the sun for friend, and for his guide a
    star;
And there's no end of voyaging when once the voice is
    heard,
For the river calls and the road calls, and oh, the call of a
    bird!

Yonder the long horizon lies, and there by night and day
The old ships draw to home again, the young ships sail
    away;
And come I may, but go I must, and if men ask you why,
You may put the blame on the stars and the sun and the
    white road and the sky!

The Wooden Horse

William F. Russell

The Wooden Horse is based on Homer's first work, the Iliad—an epic poem about the ancient war between the invading Greeks and the city of Troy. By the time The Wooden Horse begins, the struggle between the two enemies has stretched on for years. Though deeds of heroism had been done on both sides, the end of the war is still not in sight. Finally, Ulysses gets an idea.

AFTER the death of Achilles, the battles commenced once again. At times the Trojans would emerge from the gates to fight the Greeks hand-to-hand out on the plain, but these occasions were rare. Most days saw the Greeks gather at the base of the walls of Troy and try to crash the gates or scale the walls, while the Trojans, safe behind their battlements, killed many Greek warriors with their arrows and crushed others with huge stones thrown from the walls above.

After retreating yet again from a day's assault on the high-walled city, the Greeks held a council and asked advice from the prophet Calchas. Now Calchas would oftentimes see omens and portents in the activities of animals and birds, and it happened that on the previous day he had seen a hawk pursuing a dove, which hid in a hole in a rocky cliff. For a long while the hawk tried to find the hole and follow the dove into it, but he could not reach her. So he flew away for a short distance and hid himself; then the dove fluttered out into the sunlight, thinking she was no longer in danger, and the hawk swooped down on her and made his kill. The Greeks, said Calchas, ought to learn a lesson from the hawk and take Troy by cunning, for it was clear that they could not conquer her by force.

The words of Calchas inspired the wise Ulysses, and he rose to describe a trick that would allow their warriors to enter the walled city at last. The Greeks, he said, ought to make an enormous hollow horse of wood, and place the bravest men, armed for battle, inside the horse. Then all the rest of the army should embark in their ships and set sail—not to their homeland—but to a small island that lay but a short distance away. There they could conceal themselves and their ships behind the island, while the Trojans would think they had given up the battle and had sailed for home. The Trojans, he said, would come out of their city, like the dove out of her hole in the rock, and would wander about the Greek camp, and would wonder why the great wooden horse had been made and why it had been left behind. Lest they should set fire to the horse, or smash it open and discover the warriors inside, a cunning Greek, whom the Trojans did not know by sight, should be left in the camp or near it. He would tell the Trojans that the Greeks had given up all hope and had gone home, and he was to say that they feared the anger of Athena, who protected the city from harm. To soothe the goddess and to prevent her from sending violent storms to sink their ships, the Greeks (so the man was to say) had built this wooden horse as an offering to her. The Trojans, believing this story, would surely drag the horse inside the city walls. In the dark of night, then, the army would return from the nearby island, and the horse's belly would quietly issue forth the hidden warriors, who would open the city gates for their waiting comrades. Troy would be theirs at last!

The prophet was much pleased with the plan, and so on the next day, half the army was sent, axes in hand, to cut down trees and to hew thousands of planks that would shape the giant figure. In three days, the horse was finished, and Ulysses asked for brave warriors to hide inside, and for the bravest volunteer of all to stay behind and be captured by the Trojans. Then a young man called Sinon stood up and said that he would risk himself and take the chance that the Trojans might slay him outright or not believe him and burn him alive. Certainly none of the Greeks, throughout the ten years of war, had done anything more courageous, yet Sinon had never been considered a brave man. He had not fought in the front ranks, nor had he distinguished himself in any individual battles, yet there were many brave fighters among the Greeks who would not have dared to do what Sinon undertook.

The ten or twelve warriors—including the wise Ulysses and Menelaus, the husband of Helen—who climbed into the horse, first embraced their fellows as if for the last time, and then they wrapped themselves and their armor in soft silks so that no sounds would give their presence away. The rest of the army then burned all the huts along the shore and launched their ships, every man hoping that the Trojans would be so foolish as to drag the image into their town and so invite their own destruction.

From the walls the Trojans saw the black smoke go up thick

into the sky and the whole fleet of the Greeks sailing out to sea. Never were men so glad, and they armed themselves for fear of an ambush and went cautiously, sending forth scouts in front of them, down to the seashore. Here they found the huts burned down and the camp deserted, and some of the scouts also caught Sinon, who had hidden himself in a place where he was likely to be found. They rushed on him with fierce cries, and bound his hands with a rope, and kicked and dragged him along to the place where Priam and the Trojan generals were staring in wonder at the great wooden horse that had been so mysteriously left along the shore.

One of the leaders said, "It is a very curious thing. Let us drag it into the city that it may be a monument of all that we have suffered for the last ten years." But others said, "Not so; we had better burn it, or drag it out into the sea that the water may cover it, or cut it open to see whether there is anything inside."

Of these, no one was more vehement than Laocoön, one of Priam's sons and the priest of Apollo's temple at Troy. "Take heed what you do, men of Troy," he cried. "Who knows whether the Greeks have really gone away? It may be that there are armed men inside this wooden horse; it may be that it has been made so big so that warriors hidden from our sight may use it to scale our walls. No matter what its purpose may be, I fear the Greeks, even though they bear gifts." And as he spoke, he threw the spear that he had in his hand at the horse of wood, and struck it on the side. A great rattling sound was heard, and the Trojans, if they had not been so blind and foolish, might have known that there was something wrong.

While the dispute was going on, the scouts arrived with Sinon in tow, and they announced that they had found the Greek hiding not far away. Perhaps he could tell them the meaning of the giant horse of wood. The Trojans crowded around him and began to mock at him, but he cried out in a very piteous voice, "What shall I do? Where shall I go? The Greeks will not let me live, and the Trojans cry out for vengeance upon me." Then they began to pity him, and they bade him say who he was and what he had to tell.

Then the man turned to King Priam and said, "I will speak the truth, whatever may happen to me. My name is Sinon, and I will not deny that I am a Greek. Perhaps you have heard of my cousin, Palamedes, whom the Greeks called a traitor but whose only fault was that he wanted to have peace. Yes, they put him to death, and now that he is gone, they are sorry, but there is nothing they can do to bring him back. It was, in fact, because of the lies that Ulysses told against my cousin that Palamedes was accused and punished, and I swore that someday I would have revenge upon all those who wronged him. So Ulysses was always eager to do me harm, and at last, with the help of the prophet Calchas—but why do I tell you of these things? Doubtless you hold one Greek as bad as another. Kill me, if you will, only remember that my death is the very thing that Ulysses himself would give much money to secure."

Then the Trojans said, "Tell us more."

And he went on. "Many times would the Greeks have gone home, for they were very tired of the war, but the sea was so stormy that they dared not go. Then they made this great horse of wood that you see, but the storms grew worse and worse. Then they prayed to Apollo to guide them in their actions, and Apollo said, 'Men of Greece, when you came here, you first had to sacrifice the beautiful Iphigenia, daughter of Agamemnon, and so appease the winds with blood. You must appease them with blood as you leave or you will never see your homeland again.' All of us trembled at this message, for everyone feared that it might be his blood that would be sacrificed to the winds. After a while, Ulysses brought the prophet Calchas into the assembly and said, 'Tell us now who it is that the gods will have for a victim?' All the Greeks had long respected the prophecies of Calchas, and so no one guessed that he and Ulysses had secretly plotted together to seal my fate. 'Sinon is the man,' said Calchas, and all in the assembly agreed, for now Sinon's doom meant each of them was out of danger. So they fixed a day on which I was to be sacrificed, and everything was made ready. But before that day came, I broke my bonds and escaped, hiding myself in the reeds of a pond, until at last they sailed away. And now I shall never see my own country again—no, nor my wife and children—and doubtless these cruel Greeks will take vengeance on them because I escaped. And now I beseech you, O King, to have pity on me, for I have suffered much, though, indeed, I have not done harm to any man."

Then King Priam had pity on him and bade the Trojans unbind his hands, saying, "Forget your own people; from today you are one of us. But tell us now, why did the Greeks make this great horse of wood that we see?"

Then Sinon lifted up his hands to the sky and said, "O sun and moon and stars, I call you to witness that I have a good right to tell the secrets of my countrymen. Listen, O King. From the beginning, when the Greeks first came to this place, their hope resided in the help of the gods, but after ten long years of battle, they saw that they were no closer to capturing your city and returning fair Helen than they were when they first sailed to your shores. And so Agamemnon called a council of all the chiefs, and there he asked the prophet Calchas to consult the stars and omens and to reveal the will of the gods. And Calchas said to them: 'The gods have allowed us to kill many Trojan princes and to make the people cower behind their city walls, but to capture the city itself, we must go home to Greece before returning here to begin this war anew. Furthermore, we must make a horse of wood to be a peace offering to the goddess Athena. We must build it so large that the Trojans cannot take it within their walls, for if they do, Athena will never allow us to conquer the city. Nay, once the gift is within their walls, it has been foretold, the Trojans will soon lay siege to our own cities and kill our wives and children. This the gods have ordained, and also that whoever harms the horse in any way shall perish.' And my countrymen did as Calchas advised; they have gone back to Greece, but they will soon return."

This was the tale that Sinon told, and the Trojans believed it. Nor is this to be wondered at, for even the gods took part in deceiving them. And this is what they did.

While Laocoön, the priest who had thrown his spear at the great horse, was praying that his people would not bring the image into the city, the gods sent two great serpents across the sea from a nearby island. All the Trojans saw them come, with their heads raised high above the water, as is the way of certain snakes when they swim. And when they reached the land, they came on straight to where the Trojans were gathered. Their eyes were red as blood, and blazed like fire, and they made a dreadful hissing with their tongues. The Trojans grew pale with fear, and fled. But the serpents did not turn this way or that, but came straight to the altar at which Laocoön stood, with his two sons by his side. And one serpent laid hold on one of the boys, and the other on the other, and they began to devour them. Then the father picked up a sword, but before he could lash out, the serpents caught hold of him and wound themselves, two times, around his body and his neck, their heads standing in triumph high above his. And still he tried as hard as he could to tear them away with his hands, but to no avail.

And when the serpents had done their work, and both the priest and his sons were dead, then they glided to the hill on which stood the temple of Athena and hid themselves under the

101

feet of her image. And when the Trojans saw this, they said to themselves, "Now Laocoön has suffered the due reward of his deeds, for he threw his spear at the holy thing that belongs to the goddess, and now he is dead and his sons with him."

Then they all cried out together that the horse of wood should be drawn into the citadel. So they opened the great gate of the city, pulling down part of the wall so that there might be more room, and they put rollers under the feet of the horse, and they fastened ropes to it. Then they drew it into the city, boys and girls laying hold of the ropes, and singing songs with great joy. And everyone thought it a great thing if he could pull on any one of the ropes.

The rejoicing was so complete that no one gave heed to the ample signs of evil to come. Four times did the horse halt as they dragged it, before it passed through the gate, and each time there might have been heard a great clashing of metal sounds within. Also, Cassandra spoke out and prophesied that the horse would bring on the destruction of Troy. But ever since Apollo had punished her by decreeing that no one would believe her predictions again, the people refused to give any heed to her warnings. So the Trojans drew the horse of wood into the city, and that night they held a great and joyous feast to the gods, not knowing that the end of their city was now close at hand.

All through the wild festivities that night, the giant wooden horse stood in the courtyard at the very center of the city. The people of Troy danced and drank and sang songs of celebration, and even the guards who had been posted at the gates to the city joined in the revelry and drank wine until they were quite useless as sentinels. All the while, the Greek ships silently made their way from behind the island to the banks of their former camp.

Sometime after midnight, when the celebrants had either fallen asleep from drink or had gone to their homes to enjoy the first night of peace in ten years, Sinon—who had been accepted as a citizen of Troy—carefully opened the secret latch in the belly of the horse, and the Greek warriors let themselves down softly to the ground. Some rushed to the gate, killing the sleeping guards and letting in the army of the Greeks. Others sped with torches to burn the houses of the Trojan princes and to slay those who had killed their friends and brothers during the war. Terrible was the slaughter of men, unarmed and half awake, and loud were the cries of women. All through the city were the sounds of fighting and slaying and dying.

When dawn came, Troy lay in ashes, and the women were

being driven with spear shafts to the ships, and the men were left unburied, their once-noble bodies now food for wild dogs and birds. All the gold and silver, and the rich embroideries, and the ivory and amber, and the horses and chariots were divided among the army. Agamemnon was given the beautiful Cassandra, daughter of King Priam, as a prize, and lovely Helen, whose capture had begun this war ten long years ago—whose face had "launched a thousand ships and burnt the topless towers of Ilium"—was led in honor to the ship of Menelaus, and eventually back to Sparta, where she and her husband ruled as queen and king.

The Dead

Rupert Brooke

These hearts were woven of human joys and cares,
  Washed marvelously with sorrow, swift to mirth.
The years had given them kindness. Dawn was theirs,
  And sunset, and the colors of the earth.

These had seen movement, and heard music; known
  Slumber and waking; loved; gone proudly friended;
Felt the quick stir of wonder; sat alone;
  Touched flowers and furs and cheeks. All this is ended.

There are waters blown by changing winds to laughter
And lit by the rich skies, all day. And after,
  Frost, with a gesture, stays the waves that dance
And wandering loveliness. He leaves a white
  Unbroken glory, a gathered radiance,
A width, a shining peace, under the night.

Thor's Visit to Jotunheim, The Giant's Country

Thomas Bulfinch

ONE day the god Thor, with his servant Thialfi, and accompanied by Loki, set out on a journey to the giant's country. Thialfi was of all men the swiftest of foot. He bore Thor's wallet, containing their provisions. When night came on they found themselves in an immense forest, and searched on all sides for a place where they might pass the night, and at last came to a very large hall, with an entrance that took the whole breadth of one end of the building. Here they lay down to sleep, but towards midnight were alarmed by an earthquake which shook the whole edifice. Thor, rising up, called on his companions to seek with him a place of safety. On the right they found an adjoining chamber, into which the others entered, but Thor remained at the doorway with his mallet in his hand, prepared to defend himself, whatever might happen. A terrible groaning was heard during the night, and at dawn of day Thor went out and found lying near him a huge giant, who slept and snored in the way that had alarmed them so. It is said that for once Thor was afraid to use his mallet, and as the giant soon waked up, Thor contented himself with simply asking his name.

"My name is Skrymir," said the giant, "but I need not ask thy name, for I know that thou art the god Thor. But what has become of my glove?" Thor then perceived that what they had taken overnight for a hall was the giant's glove, and the chamber where his two companions had sought refuge was the thumb. Skrymir then proposed that they should travel in company, and Thor consenting, they sat down to eat their breakfast, and when they had done, Skrymir packed all the provisions into one wallet, threw it over his shoulder, and strode on before them, taking such tremendous strides that they were hard put to it to keep up with him. So they travelled the whole day, and at dusk Skrymir chose a place for them to pass the night in under a large oak tree. Skrymir then told them he would lie down to sleep. "But take ye the wallet," he added, "and prepare your supper."

Skrymir soon fell asleep and began to snore strongly; but when Thor tried to open the wallet, he found the giant had tied it up so tight he could not untie a single knot. At last Thor became wroth, and grasping his mallet with both hands he struck a furious blow on the giant's head. Skrymir, awakening, merely asked whether a leaf had not fallen on his head, and whether they had supped and were ready to go to sleep. Thor answered that they were just going to sleep, and so saying went and laid himself down under another tree. But sleep came not that night to Thor, and when Skrymir snored again so loud that the forest re-echoed with the noise, he arose, and grasping his mallet launched it with such force at the giant's skull that it made a deep dint in it. Skrymir, awakening cried out, "What's the matter? Are there any birds perched on this tree? I felt some moss from the branches fall on my head. How fares it with thee, Thor?" But Thor went away hastily, saying that he had just then awoke, and that as it was only midnight, there was still time for sleep. He, however, resolved that if he had an opportunity of striking a third blow, it should settle all matters between them. A little before daybreak he perceived that Skrymir was again fast asleep, and again grasping his mallet, he dashed it with such violence that it forced its way into the giant's skull up to the handle. But Skrymir sat up, and stroking his cheek said, "An acorn fell on my head. What! Art thou awake, Thor? Methinks it is time for us to get up and dress ourselves; but you have not now a long way before you to the city called Utgard. I have heard you whispering to one another that I am not a man of small dimensions; but if you come to Utgard you will see there many men much taller than I. Wherefore I advise you, when you come there, not to make too much of yourselves, for the followers of Utgard-Loki will not brook the boasting of such little fellows as you are. You must take the road that leads eastward, mine lies northward, so we must part here."

Hereupon he threw his wallet over his shoulders and turned away from them into the forest, and Thor had no wish to stop him or to ask for any more of his company.

Thor and his companions proceeded on their way, and towards noon descried a city standing in the middle of a plain. It was so lofty that they were obliged to bend their necks quite back on their shoulders in order to see to the top of it. On arriving they entered the city, and seeing a large palace before them with the door wide open, they went in, and found a number of men of prodigious stature, sitting on benches in the hall. Going further, they came before the king, Utgard-Loki, whom they saluted with great respect. The king, regarding them with a scornful smile, said, "If I do not mistake me, that stripling yonder must be the god Thor." Then addressing himself to Thor, he said, "Perhaps thou mayst be more than thou appearest to be. What are the feats that thou and thy fellows deem yourselves skilled in, for no one is permitted to remain here who does not, in some feat or other, excel all other men?"

"The feat that I know," said Loki, "is to eat quicker than any one else, and in this I am ready to give a proof against any one here who may choose to compete with me."

"That will indeed be a feat," said Utgard-Loki, "if thou performest what thou promisest, and it shall be tried forthwith."

He then ordered one of his men who was sitting at the farther end of the bench, and whose name was Logi, to come forward and try his skill with Loki. A trough filled with meat having been set on the hall floor, Loki placed himself at one end, and Logi at the other, and each of them began to eat as fast as he could, until they met in the middle of the trough. But it was found that Loki had only eaten the flesh, while his adversary had devoured both flesh and bone, and the trough to boot. All the company therefore adjudged that Loki was vanquished.

Utgard-Loki then asked what feat the young man who accompanied Thor could perform. Thialfi answered that he would run a race with any one who might be matched against him. The king observed that skill in running was something to boast of, but if the youth would win the match he must display great agility. He then arose and went with all who were present to a plain where there was good ground for running on, and calling a young man name Hugi, bade him run a match with Thialfi. In the first course Hugi so much outstripped his competitor that he turned back and met him not far from the starting place. Then they ran a second and a third time, but Thialfi met with no better success.

Utgard-Loki then asked Thor in what feats he would choose to give proofs of that prowess for which he was so famous. Thor answered that he would try a drinking match with any one. Utgard-Loki bade his cupbearer bring the large horn which his followers were obliged to empty when they had trespassed in any way against the law of the feast. The cupbearer having presented it to Thor, Utgard-Loki said, "Whoever is a good drinker will empty that horn at a single draught, though most men make two of it, but the most puny drinker can do it in three."

Thor looked at the horn, which seemed of no extraordinary size though somewhat long; however, as he was very thirsty, he set it to his lips, and without drawing breath, pulled as long and as deeply as he could, that he might not be obliged to make a second draft of it; but when he set the horn down and looked in, he could scarcely perceive that the liquor was diminished.

After taking breath, Thor went to it again with all his might, but when he took the horn from his mouth, it seemed to him that he had drunk rather less than before, although the horn could now be carried without spilling.

"How now, Thor?" said Utgard-Loki; "thou must not spare thyself; if thou meanest to drain the horn at the third draft thou must pull deeply; and I must needs say that thou wilt not be called so mighty a man here as thou art at home if thou showest no greater prowess in other feats than methinks will be shown in this."

Thor, full of wrath, again set the horn to his lips, and did his best to empty it; but on looking in found the liquor was only a little lower, so he resolved to make no further attempt, but gave back the horn to the cupbearer.

"I now see plainly," said Utgard-Loki, "that thou art not quite so stout as we thought thee: but wilt thou try any other feat, though methinks thou art not likely to bear any prize away with thee hence."

"What new trial hast thou to propose?" said Thor.

"We have a very trifling game here," answered Utgard-Loki, "in which we exercise none but children. It consists in merely lifting my cat from the ground; nor should I have dared to mention such a feat to the great Thor if I had not already observed that thou art by no means what we took thee for."

As he finished speaking, a large gray cat sprang on the hall floor. Thor put his hand under the cat's belly and did his utmost to raise him from the floor, but the cat, bending his back, had, notwithstanding all Thor's efforts, only one of his feet lifted up, seeing which Thor made no further attempt.

"This trial has turned out," said Utgard-Loki, "just as I imagined it would. The cat is large, but Thor is little in comparison to our men."

"Little as ye call me," answered Thor, "let me see who among you will come hither now I am in wrath and wrestle with me."

"I see no one here," said Utgard-Loki, looking at the men sitting on the benches, "who would not think it beneath him to wrestle with thee; let somebody, however, call hither that old crone, my nurse Elli, and let Thor wrestle with her if he will. She has thrown to the ground many a man not less strong than this Thor is."

A toothless old woman then entered the hall, and was told by Utgard-Loki to take hold of Thor. The tale is shortly told. The more Thor tightened his hold on the crone the firmer she stood. At length after a very violent struggle Thor began to lose his footing, and was finally brought down upon one knee. Utgard-Loki then told them to desist, adding that Thor had now no occasion to ask any one else in the hall to wrestle with him, and it was also getting late; so he showed Thor and his companions to their seats, and they passed the night there in good cheer.

The next morning, at break of day, Thor and his companions dressed themselves and prepared for their departure. Utgard-Loki ordered a table to be set for them, on which there was no lack of victuals or drink. After the repast Utgard-Loki led them to the gate of the city, and on parting asked Thor how he thought his journey had turned out, and whether he had met with any men stronger than himself. Thor told him that he could not deny but that he had brought great shame on himself. "And what grieves me most," he added, "is that ye will call me a person of little worth."

"Nay," said Utgard-Loki, "it behooves me to tell thee the truth, now thou art out of the city, which so long as I live and have my way thou shalt never enter again. And, by my troth, had I known beforehand that thou hadst so much strength in thee, and wouldst have brought me so near to a great mishap, I would not have suffered thee to enter this time. Know then that I have all along deceived thee by my illusions; first in the forest, where I tied up the wallet with iron wire so that thou couldst not untie it. After this thou gavest me three blows with thy mallet; the first, though the least, would have ended my days had it fallen on me, but I slipped aside and thy blows fell on the mountain, where thou wilt find three glens, one of them remarkably deep. These are the dints made by thy mallet. I have made use of similar illusions in the contests you have had with my followers. In the first, Loki, like hunger itself, devoured all that was set before him, but Logi was in reality nothing else than Fire, and therefore consumed not only the meat, but the trough which held it. Hugi, with whom Thialfi contended in running, was Thought, and it was impossible for Thialfi to keep pace with that. When thou in thy turn didst attempt to empty the horn, thou didst perform, by my troth, a deed so marvellous that had I not seen it myself I should never have believed it. For one end of that horn reached the sea, which thou wast not aware of, but when thou comest to the shore thou wilt perceive how much the sea has sunk by thy draughts. Thou didst perform a feat no less wonderful by lifting up the cat, and to tell thee the truth, when we saw that one of his paws was off the floor, we were all of us terror-stricken, for what thou tookest for a cat was in reality the Midgard serpent that encompasseth the earth, and he was so stretched by thee that he was barely long enough to enclose it between his head and tail. Thy wrestling with Elli was also a most astonishing feat, for there was never yet a man, nor ever will be, whom Old Age, for such in fact was Elli, will not sooner or later lay low. But now, as we are going to part, let me tell thee that it will be better for both of us if thou never come near me again, for shouldst thou do so, I shall again defend myself by other illusions, so that thou wilt only lose thy labor and get no fame from the contest with me."

On hearing these words Thor in a rage laid hold of his mallet and would have launched it at him, but Utgard-Loki had disappeared, and when Thor would have returned to the city to destroy it, he found nothing around him but a verdant plain.

The Warrior Maiden

Oneida

LONG ago, in the days before the white man came to this continent, the Oneida people were beset by their old enemies, the Mingoes. The invaders attacked the Oneida villages, stormed their palisades, set fire to their longhouses, laid waste to the land, destroyed the cornfields, killed men and boys, and abducted the women and girls. There was no resisting the Mingoes, because their numbers were like grains of sand, like pebbles on a lake shore.

The villages of the Oneida lay deserted, their fields untended, the ruins of their homes blackened. The men had taken the women, the old people, the young boys and girls into the deep forests, hiding them in secret places among rocks, in caves, and on desolate mountains. The Mingoes searched for victims, but could not find them. The Great Spirit himself helped the people to hide and shielded their places of refuge from the eyes of their enemies.

Thus the Oneida people were safe in their inaccessible retreats, but they were also starving. Whatever food they had been able to save was soon eaten up. They could either stay in their hideouts and starve, or leave them in search of food and be discovered by their enemies. The warrior chiefs and sachems met in council but could find no other way out.

Then a young girl stepped forward in the council and said that the good spirits had sent her a dream showing her how to save the Oneida. Her name was Aliquipiso and she was not afraid to give her life for her people.

Aliquipiso told the council: "We are hiding on top of a high, sheer cliff. Above us the mountain is covered with boulders and heavy sharp rocks. You warriors wait and watch here. I will go to the Mingoes and lead them to the spot at the foot of the cliff where they all can be crushed and destroyed."

The chiefs, sachems, and warriors listened to the girl with wonder. The oldest of the sachems honored her, putting around her neck strands of white and purple wampum. "The Great Spirit has blessed you, Aliquipiso, with courage and wisdom," he said. "We, your people, will always remember you."

During the night the girl went down from the heights into the forest below by way of a secret path. In the morning, Mingoe scouts found her wandering through the woods as if lost. They took her to the burned and abandoned village where she had once lived, for this was now their camp. They brought her before their warrior chief. "Show us the way to the place where your people are hiding," he commanded. "If you do this, we shall adopt you into our tribe. Then you will belong to the victors. If you refuse, you will be tortured at the stake."

"I will not show you the way," answered Aliquipiso. The Mingoes tied her to a blackened tree stump and tortured her with fire, as was their custom. Even the wild Mingoes were astonished at the courage with which the girl endured it. At last Aliquipiso pretended to weaken under the pain. "Don't hurt me any more," she cried, "I'll show you the way!"

As night came again, the Mingoes bound Aliquipiso's hands behind her back and pushed her ahead of them. "Don't try to betray us," they warned. "At any sign of it, we'll kill you." Flanked by two warriors with weapons poised, Aliquipiso led the way. Soundlessly the mass of Mingoe warriors crept behind her through thickets and rough places, over winding paths and deer trails, until at last they arrived beneath the towering cliff of sheer granite. "Come closer, Mingoe warriors," she said in a low voice, "gather around me. The Oneidas above are sleeping, thinking themselves safe. I'll show you the secret passage that leads upwards." The Mingoes crowded together in a dense mass with the girl in the center. Then Aliquipiso uttered a piercing cry: "Oneidas! The enemies are here! Destroy them!"

The Mingoes scarcely had time to strike her down before huge boulders and rocks rained upon them. There was no escape; it seemed as if the angry mountain itself were falling on them, crushing them, burying them. So many Mingoe warriors died there that the other bands of Mingoe invaders stopped pillaging the Oneida country and retired to their own hunting grounds. They never again made war on Aliquipiso's people.

The story of the girl's courage and self-sacrifice was told and retold wherever Oneidas sat around their campfires, and will be handed down from grandparent to grandchild as long as there are Oneidas on this earth.

The Great Mystery changed Aliquipiso's hair into woodbine, which the Oneidas call "running hairs" and which is a good medicine. From her body sprang honeysuckle, which to this day is known among her people as the "blood of brave women."

The Young Urashima

Helen and William McAlpine

JUST as the twilight was falling on the village of Mizunoe in the province of Tango, a fisherboy of the village called Urashima was drawing his boat up the pebbled shore after a long day at sea. Young though he was, his skill with sail, hook and line, equaled that of the best fishermen of the village; and on days when it seemed that the sea was empty of fish and his elders lamented over the poor and unsuccessful season, Urashima never failed to return without something to show for his day's labor.

One day, having secured his boat high up on the strand, Urashima started back with his catch to return home. Where the pebbles gave way to a golden stretch of sand, his attention was attracted by a noisy gesticulating circle of children, who seemed to be mercilessly flailing something in their midst. On approaching closer, Urashima found it to be a large turtle.

"It's my turn to beat the drum," cried one, and down came a stick on the turtle's back.

"It's my turn," cried another, and a stock of sea-wrack whistled through the air.

"Now, all together," they cried, and sticks and seaweed stocks rained down one after the other.

With its dazed head withdrawn under its solid shell for safety, the turtle, too slow and ponderous to escape his young tormentors, remained motionless, suffering the barbed pains that every blow darted through his shell to all parts of his body.

"What are you doing?" cried Urashima, moved to anger at their cruelty and the pitiful plight of the helpless creature. "Stop this at once! Do you think that you are good children to beat this helpless turtle?"

The children paid no heed to him and renewing their blows on the turtle's back said:

"It is no business of yours, Urashima. It is our turtle. We caught it and we can do what we like with it."

"You have no right to beat it, it feels pain just as you do. Look, if I give you money, will you let me have the turtle?" said Urashima.

"Oh! yes," they all cried at once. "If you give us money, it is yours and you can take it as quickly as you like."

Urashima handed over the money, and the children, with derisive shouts and laughing loudly at his foolishness, ran off to the village. Urashima turned to the turtle and patting its shell said:

"Well, if they had beaten you much longer, your life would have been in great danger. What brought you here, you gentle creature? From now on, please do not be so careless in the way you wander from your native sea."

Urashima took the turtle in his arms and walked with it to the seashore. Wading out knee-deep, he released it in the clear blue water and watched as it swam and plunged with delight in the waves round his feet. With a look of gratitude at its benefactor, the turtle turned seawards and swam out of sight.

It was three or four days later. The morning was warm and windless. There was no sound to be heard but the cry of a seagull gliding overhead. Urashima sat in his boat far out from land, his thoughts as listless as the line dangling on the waveless surface of the sea. All at once, he was awakened from his reverie by a voice as sweet as a temple bell calling:

"Urashima San! Urashima San!"

"Oya! Surely that's my name. It sounded as if someone was calling me. But how can it be? I am alone and out of sight of land. Indeed, I must be dreaming," thought Urashima to himself, and turned his eyes to his float again.

"Urashima San! Urashima San!" came the voice again. There could be no mistake. It was his name that was being called. He turned quickly round and there, close to his boat, its head above the glassy sea, was his friend the turtle.

"Was it you calling me just now, Turtle Chan?" asked Urashima in great surprise.

"It was indeed, my dear friend," answered the turtle. "I have come to thank you for your great kindness to me the other day and to show you my gratitude and to salute my preserver—for so I shall always regard you—with all my reverence."

"It was truly a small deed," said Urashima. "Too small to remember and not worthy of your warm gratitude. But please do not wander too far from your home. It is dangerous and there are always those who will do you injury."

"Aye! You are indeed wise, Urashima San," replied the turtle pensively. "The frog should keep to his pond and the cicada to his treetop. I was foolish. But now I have learned my lesson, and from now on I shall always keep to my ocean. Urashima San, I have something to ask you. Have you ever heard of the palace of the Dragon Princess?"

"I have heard of such a place," answered Urashima. "But nothing of the Dragon Princess, nor have I ever seen her palace."

"Then I have a great treat in store for you, Urashima San," said the turtle. "I wish to invite you to the palace of the Dragon Princess whither I will escort you on my broad back."

"Do you really mean that you know the Dragon Princess herself?" asked Urashima in great surprise.

"Not only have I the honor to know Her Highness well," replied the turtle with turtle dignity, "but I am one of her chief retainers. I told my lady how you saved my life, and she is anxious to meet you to thank you in person. So, Urashima San, will you not come?"

Urashima, still not recovered from his surprise at this strange encounter, replied with some hesitation:

"A princess of such fame, I would, of course, be honored to meet. But where is her palace? How can I get there? And does she really wish to see a lowly fisherboy like myself?"

"Urashima, my lady, as I told you, is very desirous to show her deep gratitude. She asked me to seek you out and deliver her invitation. As for getting there, do not worry. I shall take you on my back and swim with you along the lanes of the sea which lead to my lady's palace. It is a wonderful journey and we shall be there in no time. Come, Urashima!"

So saying, the turtle swam towards him, and steadied himself against the gunwale of Urashima's boat.

The turtle's words dispelled Urashima's doubts, and climbing over the side of his boat, he mounted its back. Immediately the turtle started swimming at a great pace over the waveless sea towards a pine-covered rock which seemed to have appeared at that moment, for never had Urashima seen it before. As the rock began to loom high above them, the turtle suddenly dived and moved with graceful and majestic speed into the green depths of the sea. As they plunged ever deeper, they were joined by the fair and lordly fish of the ocean.

First came a detachment of swordfish which swam far ahead, tunneling a path through the depths for the turtle and his honored passenger. Streamers of silken foam flowed in their wake and were borne in long lines by the looped tails of myriads of sea-horses. A school of dolphins followed the swordfish bearing on their backs fish from distant sea-beds whose phosphorescent scales illuminated the path with multi-colored lights. A regiment of noble sea bream flanked the sides of the procession, and above and below, in long lines, swam sardines and angel-fish, goldfish and flying fish, globefish and tunny fish, cuttle-fish and lamprey, mackerel and herring, and, surmounting all, clouds of transparent jelly-fish.

Down and down the cavalcade swam, until suddenly in a bright flash a castle appeared, lit with thousands of iridescent foam bubbles; before Urashima's eyes rose a pair of gigantic gates, glittering with brilliant colors which shimmered in the undulations of the sea, and through whose portals all manner of strange fish and creatures swam.

At the gates the turtle stopped. Settling gently on the sea-bed, it slid Urashima off its back.

"Please be so good as to wait here for a few minutes," said the turtle, and swimming through the gates, it vanished from Urashima's sight, only to return almost immediately to where the boy was sitting, absorbed in contemplation of the wonders around him.

"In the name of my gracious mistress, the Dragon Princess, I welcome you to her august palace," said the turtle in a most ceremonious voice. "My mistress waits with impatience to greet her honorable guest. Mount again on my back, Urashima San, and I will conduct you to Her Imperial presence."

Urashima climbed on to his friend's broad back, and with beating heart he was transported through the magnificent gates. Once inside, Urashima found himself in a paradise where all the rainbows of the world seemed to begin and end. Before him wavered mistily the outlines of a palace of magnificent splendor whose delicate tracery of towers, turrets, and pagodas spiralled upwards to the far world's surface. On approaching nearer, Urashima saw that what he had taken for a profusion of golden blooms and blossoms were rows of beautiful maidens, attired in rich brocade dresses, and each with a page, no less beautiful than his mistress, to attend her and to sway the ornamented fan above her head. On looking closer, he saw that each maiden wore bright bands of sea-grass and anemones among her high-piled tresses; and nestling in the waves of the hair at the front was a young sea bream, while twined among the topknots of the pages small squibs and octopuses wriggled their tenuous limbs.

As Urashima stood in rapt wonder, the lines of attendants parted like a wave in the center to reveal a young woman of godly beauty who moved slowly towards him. It was the far-famed and legendary Princess Oto, the Dragon Princess. Urashima fell to his knees and bowed deeply.

"You are welcome to my humble dwelling," said the princess, "more perhaps than anyone in the kingdom of my sea and beyond it. For you saved the life of my dear and esteemed retainer, and I owe you an eternal debt of gratitude. I and my people will rejoice, if you will honor us with your company for as long as you may stay."

Urashima bowed deeply again. Then rising to his feet, he walked with the princess along the great corridors of the palace followed by the maidens and attendants. The floors were covered in agate, from which rose coral columns to support the curved roofs and ceiling of coral tracery. From the alcoves along the corridors came strains of music which followed them as they passed; and the waters everywhere were scented with the richest of perfumes. In the room which they finally entered there was a low red table covered with a cloth of richest damask, and two carved chairs of the same vivid red wood.

The princess proceeded before Urashima and sat with queenly grace in one of them. She motioned Urashima to the place beside her.

"You must be hungry, Urashima San, after your long journey; so let us eat," said the princess, and gestured in command to one of the attendants.

Immediately from between the coral columns came a long line of other attendants, bearing before them on trays of gold lacquer rich dishes from the four corners of the ocean. While they ate, maidens performed dances from the courts of kings of ancient times, and sang melodies of love from tales of old romances to the accompaniment of harp, flute, and drum.

The meal ended, the princess invited Urashima to accompany her on a tour of the palace. They passed through rooms with walls of ivory and blue marble, jade and amber, sandal-wood and cedarwood, and floors of stone from the quarries of distant seas whose colors glowed and fused with the rich hues of the walls. And carved on the ceiling of every room was the magnificent gold and red dragon of Princess Oto's house.

At last they came to a room overlooking a curving red bridge which hung over a stream, deep and crystal clear. Here the princess paused, and standing near one of the sliding screen windows, said:

"Pray, rest awhile, and I will show you the scenery of the four seasons in the space of a few moments. First, we shall look through the eastern window."

The princess slid back the delicate screen, and before him Urashima saw a landscape in all the freshness and greenness of spring. A haze hung over a grove of cherry trees whose buds were already coming into bloom. Willows wept over the waters of the stream, and from every branch came the song of the little bush-warbler. Urashima's only wish was to be left here forever, but the princess drew him to the southern window, and opening it, bade him look.

Suddenly summer in all its warmth broke forth. Fragrant hosts of white gardenia blossoms encircled a pond, whose surface was covered with floating lilies of every shade, their petals hung with quicksilver beads of dew. Jewel-plumaged water-fowl darted over the surface, bringing the dewdrops down in a tingling cascade as their wings brushed the petals. Cicadas filled the air with their songs, and frogs croaked in lazy contentment. But now the princess again drew Urashima away and bade him look through the western window.

Before him, the landscape unfolded into the distance and was afire with the autumn red of the maple tree. On mountain and hill, by lake and river, in valley and plain, the earth was laid with a carpet of flames. A mackerel sky hung over the mountain peaks, and the waters of the river and the lake glowed red in the autumn air. And, strangely, the odor of chrysanthemums pervaded the scene, but no blooms could be seen. Urashima, lost in wonderment, was brought to himself again by the voice of the princess who asked him to come to the northern window. As she drew the screens apart, Urashima became spellbound.

It was winter, and everywhere the world lay hushed under a mantle of snow. Twilight floated over the frozen pond, where, single-limbed, the cranes stood in sleep. Bullrushes and reeds crackled in a wind that suddenly rose and died. Tree, bush, and shrub were bloomed with snow, and spikes of frost hung from branch and leaf. Antlered deer idled under the cold, erect pines, and bears, dark brown against the winter white, were having their evening meal of bark.

Urashima's delight knew no bounds. All thought of returning home left his heart; his only wish was to remain forever with Princess Oto in her charmed, magic fairyland. Month after month Urashima lived in this enchantment. Each day brought forth some new marvel to delight him, and each night some new miracle to entertain him. How long he stayed he did not know, nor did he care. But quite suddenly thoughts of his parents began to trouble him. He grew quiet and sad, quite different from the gay and happy youth he had been. One day the princess asked gently:

"Urashima Sama, why are you so sad and distant from me? What has happened to you? Can we no longer give you pleasure?" But Urashima turned his face away and would not answer.

The princess, much troubled, sought every day to produce newer delights and greater pleasures for him, but all to no avail. No matter how delicate the rare foods, how divinely sweet the voices of the singers, how graceful the dancers or bewitching the princess, Urashima refused to be comforted. At last, after the princess had again begged him to tell her his troubles, Urashima held his sleeve before his eyes and answered:

"For some time past I have been troubled by dreams of my parents. I fear for their welfare and I would dearly love to see them."

At this the princess wept bitterly and Urashima, himself deeply moved, took her hand in his and said:

"Do not weep! I wish only to reassure myself that all is well with them. Only allow me to visit them for a brief while, and I shall return to live happily with you forever."

The princess was overcome with grief; but seeing Urashima's unhappiness, she knew that it would become greater if she detained him.

"Urashima Sama, grief-stricken though I am, I understand. Please go to them. But before you start, I have something for you which you must take with you."

With these words the princess disappeared into an inner room, but returned almost at once carrying a beautiful gold-leafed lacquer box tied with tasselled red cords. Bowing deeply, she placed the box before Urashima, who took it in both hands and held it to his head as a token of his acceptance.

"Urashima Sama, this is a special, a very special box," said Princess Oto. "It contains a treasure of untold value, but one which is best left undisturbed by prying eyes. We call it a 'sayonara gift,' and here I give it to you and wish with all my heart for your speedy return. Go at once, Urashima, and we shall wait longingly for you to come back."

The princess bowed again and withdrew a few steps, hiding her eyes behind her long sleeves and unable to restrain her tears.

Urashima, too, was sad at the thought of leaving his beautiful princess, but knowing that it would be unmanly to show his feelings before her, he answered bravely:

"I will go, my princess. Your farewell gift I will jealously guard until my return. My eyes will never look upon its contents. My only longing will be to see your dear face again."

He gazed on the box with such intensity that the princess knew he was fighting to restrain his own tears.

"One day you will return to me, Urashima Sama," said the princess, "and I shall always be waiting for that day. Take good care of my gift and it will bring you back safely to your home under the sea. But remember, Urashima Sama, do not, for your sake and my sake, ever open the box. It breaks my heart to think of what will happen should you disobey my warning. Let these be my last words to you, Urashima Sama. Farewell!"

The princess was too distressed to see him to the gates. She remained where she was and watched him walk slowly out of the room to where his friend the turtle was patiently waiting. With the box held firmly under his arm, Urashima mounted the turtle's back and they swam slowly through the green depths. Urashima gazed with longing and sadness upon the place which held everything most dear to him, until it grew dimmer and finally disappeared.

Soon the greenness gave place to deep blue, and all at once they rose to the surface on the crest of a large wave which carried them forward at a great speed. In silence they sped along, until at last they came in sight of a low, sandy beach. Urashima's heart suddenly lifted; for here, at last, was home. What a welcome he would have! What wonders he had to recount! The turtle swam to the shallows where Urashima could easily dismount from his back. While he stood in the water, his gift held tightly in his arms, the turtle gently backed away, saying as he went:

"Urashima Sama! *Sayonara! Sayonara!* Please take good care of yourself and I shall be waiting patiently to take you back to your home under the sea. *Sayonara*, Urashima Sama!"

The turtle turned his great body round, and without a further word or look, swam swiftly away.

Urashima watched until his dear friend disappeared into the distance. His heart was heavy and a deep melancholy came over him. He turned to look at his familiar homeland with a subdued spirit. To his great surprise everything had changed and there was not a landmark he could recognize. In bewilderment he walked up from the beach and into the village street. It hardly seemed the same. The temple still stood on the hill, but old familiar houses had been torn down and new ones had been built. The wayside shrine was still at the entrance of the village, but a new road had been cut and a new wooden bridge spanned the river. Everywhere strange faces regarded him with curiosity, and not an old friend could he see. He hastened along the street towards his parents' home, but stood bewildered when he saw it. It was overgrown with weeds; uncut grass grew in tufts where the bamboo gate once stood; the thatched roof was in decay and the walls were crumbling in ruins.

"What has happened?" muttered Urashima as he looked around him. "Is this my parents' home? Is this my native village? How could this desolation come about in such a short time? Where are my parents?"

At this moment an old woman, whose back was bent parallel to the road, came limping towards him, and Urashima stopped before her.

"Grandma! Where is Urashima's home? Where have his people gone? What has become of them? Please tell me!" he pleaded.

The old woman screwed her head round to peer at Urashima. She looked at him for a long time, and then said:

"Eh! Urashima, you say? Never heard of such a name. I have lived her for over eighty years and I've never come across anyone of that name."

Urashima became very agitated and said loudly:

"But this is where they used to live. And no one knows better than I. Surely you must have heard of them."

The old woman settled her old body down by the roadside and remained silent for some time. Many things seemed to be struggling in her wizened head. At last she nodded and muttered to Urashima:

"Urashima! Urashima! That was the name I heard as a child, I believe. Was he not the boy who went over the sea on a big turtle's back and never returned? Wasn't that the boy of the legend? It is said that he was taken to the Dragon Palace and there he remained a prisoner. But I don't know. It all happened so long ago. I heard the story as a child, as I said, and the story goes that it all happened over three hundred years ago."

Urashima could hardly contain his astonishment and his sorrow as he realized what had happened.

"Three hundred years ago! Three hundred years ago!" Urashima muttered to himself. "Three years only I thought I stayed, but now it seems that for every year I dreamed, a hundred years passed by. That explains all: my parents dead; our house in ruins; the village not recognizable. Oh! what have I done!" And he wept bitterly in his sorrow.

After a time, his thoughts turned to his princess and to his new home under the sea. There was his only hope. There was his only happiness. He ran frantically back to the beach and scanned the sea for a sign of the turtle. But nowhere was it to be seen.

"Turtle San! Turtle San! Where are you? I want to return at once. Come to me!" he cried. But only the sighing of the retreating sea through the shallows answered him. He sat down in despair and put the lacquered box, which all this time he had been clutching under his arm, beside him. At the sight of it, he suddenly cried in joy:

"Surely her gift will help me? Surely there are instructions inside the box which will tell me how to return to my dear princess."

Forgetting the princess's warning, he eagerly untied the tassels and with trembling hands lifted the lid. A cloud of purple mist rose from the box and enveloped him in its folds. As it cleared away, Urashima, to his horror, felt a terrible change come over him. His fresh young face fell into countless lines and wrinkles; his bright eyes became dimmed and bleary; his hair turned snow-white and thin. Cramp overcame his fingers and pains his legs, now thin and shot with thick veins. He tried to rise, but countless years racked his whole body, and he found himself staring into the sand, for his back was bent at right angles like the old woman's and he could not straighten it.

"Oh! what have I done? What have I done? I forgot your words, my dear princess, and rashly opened the box. Now I know why you warned me. You sealed my youth into this box and I alone have lost it. Now all is gone, all is gone," he cried. Tears streamed down his cheeks. Through his almost sightless eyes he gazed at the sea, but there was nothing to be seen, and only the sea itself cried with him in his sorrow.

Riddles in the Dark

from The Hobbit

J.R.R. Tolkien

Against his better judgment, Bilbo Baggins, the hobbit, joins the company of Gandalf, the wizard, and thirteen dwarves. They travel toward the ruins of an ancient dwarven kingdom to confront the fierce dragon, Smaug. However, the party is soon captured by the foul, misshapen goblins and dragged underground to face the terrible goblin king. Escaping, they run through dark tunnels, where Bilbo hits his head on a protruding rock and knocks himself unconscious. Unaware of the hobbit's fate, Gandalf and the dwarves continue to flee, leaving Bilbo behind.

WHEN Bilbo opened his eyes, he wondered if he had; for it was just as dark as with them shut. No one was anywhere near him. Just imagine his fright! He could hear nothing, see nothing, and he could feel nothing except the stone of the floor.

Very slowly he got up and groped about on all fours, till he touched the wall of the tunnel; but neither up nor down it could he find anything: nothing at all, no sign of goblins, no sign of dwarves. His head was swimming, and he was far from certain even of the direction they had been going in when he had his fall. He guessed as well as he could, and crawled along for a good way, till suddenly his hand met what felt like a tiny ring of cold metal lying on the floor of the tunnel. It was a turning point in his career, but he did not know it. He put the ring in his pocket almost without thinking; certainly it did not seem of any particular use at the moment. He did not go much further, but sat down on the cold floor and gave himself up to complete miserableness, for a long while. He thought of himself frying bacon and eggs in his own kitchen at home—for he could feel inside that it was high time for some meal or other; but that only made him miserabler.

He could not think what to do; nor could he think what had happened; or why he had been left behind; or why, if he had been left behind, the goblins had not caught him; or even why his head was so sore. The truth was he had been lying quiet, out of sight and out of mind, in a very dark corner for a long while.

After some time he felt for his pipe. It was not broken, and that was something. Then he felt for his pouch, and there was some tobacco in it, and that was something more. Then he felt for matches and he could not find any at all, and that shattered his hopes completely. Just as well for him, as he agreed when he came to his senses. Goodness knows what the striking of matches and the smell of tobacco would have brought on him out of dark holes in that horrible place. Still at the moment he felt very crushed. But in slapping all his pockets and feeling all round himself for matches his hand came on the hilt of his little sword—the little dagger that he got from the trolls, and that he had quite forgotten; nor do the goblins seem to have noticed it, as he wore it inside his breeches.

Now he drew it out. It shone pale and dim before his eyes. "So it is an elvish blade, too," he thought; "and goblins are not very near, and yet not far enough."

But somehow he was comforted. It was rather splendid to be wearing a blade made in Gondolin for the goblin-wars of which so many songs had sung; and also he had noticed that such weapons made a great impression on goblins that came upon them suddenly.

"Go back?" he thought. " No good at all! Go sideways? Impossible! Go Forward? Only thing to do! On we go!" So up he got, and trotted along with his little sword held in front of him and one hand feeling the wall, and his heart all of a patter and a pitter.

Now certainly Bilbo was in what is called a tight place. But you must remember it was not quite so tight for him as it would have been for me or for you. Hobbits are not quite like ordinary people; and after all if their holes are nice cheery places and properly aired, quite different from the tunnels of the goblins, still they are more used to tunnelling than we are, and they do not easily lose their sense of direction underground—not when their heads have recovered from being bumped. Also they can move very quietly, and hide easily, and recover wonderfully from falls and bruises, and they have a fund of wisdom and wise sayings that men have mostly never heard or have forgotten long ago.

I should not have liked to have been in Mr. Baggins' place, all the same. The tunnel seemed to have no end. All he knew was that it was still going down pretty steadily and keeping in the same direction in spite of a twist and a turn or two. There were passages leading off to the side every now and then, as he knew by the glimmer of his sword, or could feel with his hand on the wall. Of these he took no notice, except to hurry past for fear of goblins or half-imagined dark things coming out of them. On and on he went, and down and down; and still he heard no sound of anything except the occasional whirr of a bat by his ears, which startled him at first, till it became too frequent to bother about. I do not know how long he kept on like this, hating to go on, not daring to stop, on, on, until he was tireder than tired. It seemed like all the way to tomorrow and over it to the days beyond.

Suddenly without any warning he trotted splash into water! Ugh! it was icy cold. That pulled him up sharp and short. He did not know whether it was just a pool in the path, or the edge of an underground stream that crossed the passage, or the brink of a deep dark subterranean lake. The sword was hardly shining at all. He stopped, and he could hear, when he listened hard, drops drip-drip-dripping from an unseen roof into the water below; but there seemed no other sort of sound.

"So it is a pool or a lake, and not an underground river," he thought. Still he did not dare to wade out into the darkness. He could not swim; and he thought, too, of nasty slimy things, with big bulging blind eyes, wriggling in the water. There are strange things living in the pools and lakes in the hearts of mountains: fish whose fathers swam in, goodness only knows how many years ago, and never swam out again, while their eyes grew bigger and bigger and bigger from trying to see in the blackness; also there are other things more slimy than fish. Even in the tunnels and caves the goblins have made for themselves there are other things living unbeknown to them that have sneaked in from outside to lie up in the dark. Some of these caves, too, go back in their beginnings to ages before the goblins, who only widened them and joined them up with passages, and the original owners are still there in odd corners, slinking and nosing about.

Deep down here by the dark water lived old Gollum, a small slimy creature. I don't know where he came from, nor who or what he was. He was Gollum—as dark as darkness, except for two big round pale eyes in his thin face. He had a little boat, and he rowed about quite quietly on the lake; for lake it was, wide and deep and deadly cold. He paddled it with large feet dangling over the side, but never a ripple did he make. Not he. He was looking out of his pale lamp-like eyes for blind fish, which he grabbed with his long fingers as quick as thinking. He liked meat too. Goblin he thought good, when he could get it;

but he took care they never found him out. He just throttled them from behind, if they ever came down alone anywhere near the edge of the water, while he was prowling about. They very seldom did, for they had a feeling that something unpleasant was lurking down there, down at the very roots of the mountain. They had come on the lake, when they were tunnelling down long ago, and they found they could go no further; so there their road ended in that direction, and there was no reason to go that way—unless the Great Goblin sent them. Sometimes he took a fancy for fish from the lake, and sometimes neither goblin nor fish came back.

Actually Gollum lived on a slimy island of rock in the middle of the lake. He was watching Bilbo now from the distance with his pale eyes like telescopes. Bilbo could not see him, but he was wondering a lot about Bilbo, for he could see that he was no goblin at all.

Gollum go into his boat and shot off from the island, while Bilbo was sitting on the brink altogether flummoxed and at the end of his way and his wits. Suddenly up came Gollum and whispered and hissed:

"Bless us and splash us, my precioussss! I guess it's a choice feast; at least a tasty morsel it'd make us, gollum!" And when he said *gollum* he made a horrible swallowing noise in his throat. That is how he got his name, though he always called himself 'my precious.'

The hobbit jumped nearly out of his skin when the hiss came in his ears, and he suddenly saw the pale eyes sticking out at him.

"Who are you?" he said, thrusting his dagger in front of him.

"What iss he, my preciouss?" whispered Gollum (who always spoke to himself through never having anyone else to speak to). This is what he had come to find out, for he was not really very hungry at the moment, only curious; otherwise he would have grabbed first and whispered afterwards.

"I am Mr. Bilbo Baggins. I have lost the dwarves and I have lost the wizard, and I don't know where I am; and I don't want to know, if only I can get away."

"What's he got in his handses?" said Gollum, looking at the sword, which he did not quite like.

"A sword, a blade which came out of Gondolin!"

"Sssss," said Gollum, and became quite polite. "Praps ye sits here and chats with it a bitsy, my preciousss. It like riddles, praps it does, does it?" He was anxious to appear friendly, at any rate for the moment, and until he found out more about the sword and the hobbit, whether he was quite alone really, whether he was good to eat, and whether Gollum was really hungry. Riddles were all he could think of. Asking them, and sometimes guessing them, had been the only game he had ever played with other funny creatures sitting in their holes in the long, long ago, before he lost all his friends and was driven away, alone, and crept down, down, into the dark under the mountains.

"Very well," said Bilbo, who was anxious to agree, until he found out more about the creature, whether he was quite alone, whether he was fierce or hungry, and whether he was a friend of the goblins.

"You ask first," he said, because he had not had time to think of a riddle.

So Gollum hissed:

> *What has roots as nobody sees,*
> *Is taller than trees,*
> > *Up, up it goes,*
> > *And yet never grows?*

"Easy!" said Bilbo. "Mountain, I suppose."

"Does it guess easy? It must have a competition with us, my preciouss! If precious asks, and it doesn't answer, we eats it, my preciousss. If it asks us, and we doesn't answer, then we does what it wants, eh? We shows it the way out, yes!"

"All right!" said Bilbo, not daring to disagree, and nearly bursting his brain to think of riddles that could save him from being eaten.

> *Thirty white horses on a red hill,*
> > *First they champ,*
> > *Then they stamp,*
> *Then they stand still.*

That was all he could think of to ask—the idea of eating was rather on his mind. It was rather an old one, too, and Gollum knew the answer as well as you do.

"Chestnuts, chestnuts," he hissed. "Teeth! teeth! my preciousss; but we has only six!" Then he asked his second:

> *Voiceless it cries,*
> *Wingless flutters,*
> *Toothless bites,*
> *Mouthless mutters.*

"Half a moment!" cried Bilbo, who was still thinking uncomfortably about eating. Fortunately he had once heard something rather like this before, and getting his wits back he thought of the answer. "Wind, wind of course," he said, and he was so pleased that he made up one on the spot. "This'll puzzle the nasty little underground creature," he thought:

> An eye in a blue face
> Saw an eye in a green face.
> "That eye is like to this eye"
> Said the first eye,
> "But in low place,
> Not in high place."

"Ss, ss, ss," said Gollum. He had been underground a long long time, and was forgetting this sort of thing. But just as Bilbo was beginning to hope that the wretch would not be able to answer, Gollum brought up memories of ages and ages and ages before, when he lived with his grandmother in a hole in a bank by a river, "Sss, sss, my preciouss," he said. "Sun on the daisies it means, it does."

But these ordinary aboveground everyday sort of riddles were tiring for him. Also they reminded him of days when he had been less lonely and sneaky and nasty, and that put him out of temper. What is more they made him hungry; so this time he tried something a bit more difficult and more unpleasant:

> It cannot be seen, cannot be felt,
> Cannot be heard, cannot be smelt.
> It lies behind stars and under hills,
>   And empty holes it fills.
> It comes first and follows after,
>   Ends life, kills laughter.

Unfortunately for Gollum Bilbo had heard that sort of thing before; and the answer was all round him anyway. "Dark!" he said without even scratching his head or putting on his thinking cap.

> A box without hinges, key, or lid,
> Yet golden treasure inside is hid,

he asked to gain time, until he could think of a really hard one. This he thought a dreadfully easy chestnut, though he had not asked it in the usual words. But it proved a nasty poser for Gollum. He hissed to himself, and still he did not answer; he whispered and spluttered.

After some while Bilbo became impatient. "Well, what is it?" he said. "The answer's not a kettle boiling over, as you seem to think from the noise you are making."

"Give us a chance; let it give us a chance, my preciouss—ss—ss."

"Well," said Bilbo, after giving him a long chance, "what about your guess?"

But suddenly Gollum remembered thieving from nests long ago, and sitting under the river bank teaching his grandmother, teaching his grandmother to suck—"Eggses!" he hissed. "Eggses it is!" Then he asked:

> *Alive without breath,*
> *As cold as death;*
> *Never thirsty, ever drinking,*
> *All in mail never clinking.*

He also in his turn thought this was a dreadfully easy one, because he was always thinking of the answer. But he could not remember anything better at the moment, he was so flustered by the egg-question. All the same it was a poser for poor Bilbo, who never had anything to do with the water if he could help it. I imagine you know the answer, of course, or can guess it as easy as winking, since you are sitting comfortably at home and have not the danger of being eaten to disturb your thinking. Bilbo sat and cleared his throat once or twice, but no answer came.

After a while Gollum began to hiss with pleasure to himself: "Is it nice, my preciousss? Is it juicy? Is it scrumptiously crunchable?" He began to peer at Bilbo out of the darkness.

"Half a moment," said the hobbit shivering. "I gave you a good long chance just now."

"It must make haste, haste!" said Gollum, beginning to climb out of his boat on to the shore to get at Bilbo. But when he put his long webby foot in the water, a fish jumped out in a fright and fell on Bilbo's toes.

"Ugh!" he said, "it is cold and clammy!"—and so he guessed. "Fish! Fish!" he cried. "It is fish!"

Gollum was dreadfully disappointed; but Bilbo asked another riddle as quick as ever he could, so that Gollum had to get back into his boat and think.

No-legs lay on one-leg, two-legs sat near on three-legs, four-legs got some.

It was not really the right time for this riddle, but Bilbo was in a hurry. Gollum might have had some trouble guessing it, if he had asked it at another time. As it was, talking of fish, "no-legs" was not so very difficult, and after that the rest was easy. "Fish on a little table, man at table sitting on a stool, the cat has the bones"—that of course is the answer, and Gollum soon gave it. Then he thought the time had come to ask something hard and horrible. This is what he said:

This thing all things devours:
Birds, beasts, trees, flowers;
Gnaws iron, bites steel;
Grinds hard stones to meal;
Slays king, ruins town,
And beats high mountain down.

Poor Bilbo sat in the dark thinking of all the horrible names of all the giants and ogres he had ever heard told of in tales, but not one of them had done all these things. He had a feeling that the answer was quite different and that he ought to know it, but he could not think of it. He began to get frightened, and that is bad for thinking. Gollum began to get out of his boat. He flapped into the water and paddled to the bank; Bilbo could see his eyes coming towards him. His tongue seemed to stick in his mouth; he wanted to shout out: "Give me more time! Give me time!" But all that came out with a sudden squeal was:

"Time! Time!"

Bilbo was saved by pure luck. For that of course was the answer.

Gollum was disappointed once more; and now he was getting angry, and also tired of the game. It had made him very hungry indeed. This time he did not go back to the boat. He sat down in the dark by Bilbo. That made the hobbit most dreadfully uncomfortable and scattered his wits.

"It's got to ask uss a quesstion, my preciouss, yes, yess, yesss. Jusst one more quesstion to guess, yes, yess," said Gollum.

But Bilbo simply could not think of any question with that nasty wet cold thing sitting next to him, and pawing and poking him. He scratched himself, he pinched himself; still he could not think of anything.

"Ask us! ask us!" said Gollum.

Bilbo pinched himself and slapped himself; he gripped on his little sword; he even felt in his pocket with his other hand. There he found the ring he had picked up in the passage and forgotten about.

"What have I got in my pocket?" he said aloud. He was talking to himself, but Gollum thought it was a riddle, and he was frightfully upset.

"Not fair! not fair!" he hissed. "It isn't fair, my precious, is it, to ask us what it's got in its nassty little pocketses?"

Bilbo seeing what had happened and having nothing better to ask stuck to his question. "What have I got in my pocket?" he said louder.

"S-s-s-s-s," hissed Gollum. "It must give us three guesseses, my preciouss, three guesseses."

"Very well! Guess away!" said Bilbo.

"Handses!" said Gollum.

"Wrong," said Bilbo, who had luckily just taken his hand out again. "Guess again!"

"S-s-s-s-s," said Gollum more upset than ever. He thought of all the things he kept in his own pockets: fishbones, goblins' teeth, wet shells, a bit of bat-wing, a sharp stone to sharpen his fangs on, and other nasty things. He tried to think what other people kept in their pockets.

"Knife!" he said at last.

"Wrong!" said Bilbo, who had lost his some time ago. "Last guess!"

Now Gollum was in a much worse state than when Bilbo had asked him the egg-question. He hissed and spluttered and rocked himself backwards and forwards, and slapped his feet on the floor, and wriggled and squirmed; but still he did not dare to waste his last guess.

"Come on!" said Bilbo. "I am waiting!" He tried to sound bold and cheerful, but he did not feel at all sure how the game was going to end, whether Gollum guessed right or not.

"Time's up!" he said.

"String, or nothing!" shrieked Gollum, which was not quite fair—working in two guesses at once.

"Both wrong," cried Bilbo very much relieved; and he jumped at once to his feet, put his back to the nearest wall, and held out his little sword. He knew, of course, that the riddle-game

was sacred and of immense antiquity, and even wicked creatures were afraid to cheat when they played at it. But he felt he
could not trust this slimy thing to keep any promise at a pinch.
Any excuse would do for him to slide out of it. And after all that
last question had not been a genuine riddle according to the ancient laws.

But at any rate Gollum did not at once attack him. He could
see the sword in Bilbo's hand. He sat still, shivering and whispering. At last Bilbo could wait no longer.

"Well?" he said. "What about your promise? I want to go. You
must show me the way."

"Did we say so, precious? Show the nassty little Baggins the
way out, yes, yes. But what has it got in its pocketses, eh? Not
string, precious, but not nothing. Oh no! gollum!"

"Never you mind," said Bilbo. "A promise is a promise."

"Cross it is, impatient, precious," hissed Gollum. "But it must
wait, yes it must. We can't go up the tunnels so hasty. We must
go and get some things first, yes, things to help us."

"Well, hurry up!" said Bilbo, relieved to think of Gollum going
away. He thought he was just making an excuse and did not mean
to come back. What was Gollum talking about? What useful thing
could he keep out on the dark lake? But he was wrong. Gollum
did mean to come back. He was angry now and hungry. And he
was a miserable wicked creature, and already he had a plan.

Not far away was his island, of which Bilbo knew nothing,
and there in his hiding-place he kept a few wretched oddments,
and one very beautiful thing, very beautiful, very wonderful. He
had a ring, a golden ring, a precious ring.

"My birthday-present!" he whispered to himself, as he had
often done in the endless dark days. "That's what we wants
now, yes; we wants it!"

He wanted it because it was a ring of power, and if you
slipped that ring on your finger, you were invisible; only in the
full sunlight could you be seen, and then only by your shadow,
and that would be shaky and faint.

"My birthday-present! It came to me on my birthday, my precious," So he had always said to himself. But who knows how
Gollum came by that present, ages ago in the old days when
such rings were still at large in the world? Perhaps even the
Master who ruled them could not have said. Gollum used to
wear it at first, till it tired him; and then he kept it in a pouch
next his skin, till it galled him; and now usually he hid it in a
hole in the rock on his island, and was always going back to

look at it. And still sometimes he put it on, when he could not bear to be parted from it any longer, or when he was very, very, hungry, and tired of fish. Then he would creep along dark passages looking for stray goblins. He might even venture into places where the torches were lit and made his eyes blink and smart; for he would be safe. Oh yes, quite safe. No one would see him, no one would notice him, till he had his fingers on their throat. Only a few hours ago he had worn it, and caught a small goblin-imp. How it squeaked! He still had a bone or two left to gnaw, but he wanted something softer.

"Quite safe, yes," he whispered to himself. "It won't see us, will it, my precious? No. It won't see us, and its nassty little sword will be useless, yes quite."

That is what was in his wicked little mind, as he slipped suddenly from Bilbo's side, and flapped back to his boat, and went off into the dark. Bilbo thought he had heard the last of him. Still he waited a while; for he had no idea how to find his way out alone.

Suddenly he heard a screech. It sent a shiver down his back. Gollum was cursing and wailing away in the gloom, not very far off by the sound of it. He was on his island, scrabbling here and there, searching and seeking in vain.

"Where is it? Where iss it?" Bilbo heard him crying. "Losst it is, my precious, lost, lost! Curse us and crush us, my precious is lost!"

"What's the matter?" Bilbo called. "What have you lost?"

"It mustn't ask us," shrieked Gollum. "Not its business, no, gollum! It's losst, gollum, gollum, gollum."

"Well, so am I," cried Bilbo, "and I want to get unlost. And I won the game, and you promised. So come along! Come and let me out, and then go on with your looking!" Utterly miserable as Gollum sounded, Bilbo could not find much pity in his heart, and he had a feeling that anything Gollum wanted so much could hardly be something good. "Come along!" he shouted.

"No, not yet, precious!" Gollum answered. "We must search for it, it's lost, gollum."

"But you never guessed my last question, and you promised," said Bilbo.

"Never guessed!" said Gollum. Then suddenly out of the gloom came a sharp hiss. "What has it got in its pocketses? Tell us that. It must tell first."

As far as Bilbo knew, there was no particular reason why he should not tell. Gollum's mind had jumped to a guess quicker than his; naturally, for Gollum had brooded for ages on this one thing, and he was always afraid of its being stolen. But Bilbo was annoyed at the delay. After all, he had won the game, pretty fairly, at a horrible risk. "Answers were to be guessed not given," he said.

"But it wasn't a fair question," said Gollum. "Not a riddle, precious, no."

"Oh well, if it's a matter of ordinary questions," Bilbo replied, "then I asked one first. What have you lost? Tell me that!"

"What has it got in its pocketses?" The sound came hissing louder and sharper, and as he looked towards it, to his alarm Bilbo now saw two small points of light peering at him. As suspicion grew in Gollum's mind, the light of his eyes burned with a pale flame.

"What have you lost?" Bilbo persisted.

But now the light in Gollum's eyes had become a green fire, and it was coming swiftly nearer. Gollum was in his boat again, paddling wildly back to the dark shore; and such a rage of loss and suspicion was in his heart that no sword had any more terror for him.

Bilbo could not guess what had maddened the wretched creature, but he saw that all was up, and that Gollum meant to murder him at any rate. Just in time he turned and ran blindly back up the dark passage down which he had come, keeping close to the wall and feeling it with his left hand.

"What has it got in its pocketses?" he heard the hiss loud behind him, and the splash as Gollum leapt from his boat. "What have I, I wonder?" he said to himself, as he panted and stumbled along. He put his left hand in his pocket. The ring felt very cold as it quietly slipped on to his groping forefinger.

The hiss was close behind him. He turned now and saw Gollum's eyes like small green lamps coming up the slope. Terrified he tried to run faster, but suddenly he struck his toes on a snag in the floor, and fell flat with his little sword under him.

In a moment Gollum was on him. But before Bilbo could do anything, recover his breath, pick himself up, or wave his sword, Gollum passed by, taking no notice of him, cursing and whispering as he ran.

What could it mean? Gollum could see in the dark. Bilbo could see the light of his eyes palely shining even from behind. Painfully he got up, and sheathed his sword, which was now glowing faintly gain, then very cautiously he followed. There seemed nothing else to do. It was no good crawling back down to Gollum's water. Perhaps if he followed him, Gollum might lead him to some way of escape without meaning to.

"Curse it! curse it! curse it!" hissed Gollum. "Curse the Baggins! It's gone! What has it got in its pocketses? Oh we guess, we guess, my precious. He's found it, yes he must have. My birthday-present."

Bilbo pricked up his ears. He was at last beginning to guess himself. He hurried a little, getting as close as he dared behind Gollum, who was still going quickly, not looking back, but turning his head from side to side, as Bilbo could see from the faint glimmer on the walls.

"My birthday-present! Curse it! How did we lose it, my precious? Yes, that's it. When we came this way last, when we twisted that nassty young squeaker. That's it. Curse it! It slipped from us, after all these ages and ages! It's gone, gollum."

Suddenly Gollum sat down and began to weep, a whistling and gurgling sound horrible to listen to. Bilbo halted and flattened himself against the tunnel-wall. After a while Gollum stopped weeping and began to talk. He seemed to be having an argument with himself.

"It's no good going back there to search, no. We doesn't remember all the places we've visited. And it's no use. The Baggins has got it in its pocketses; the nassty noser has found it, we says."

"We guesses, precious, only guesses. We can't know till we find the nassty creature and squeezes it. But it doesn't know what the present can do, does it? It'll just keep it in its pocketses. It doesn't know, and it can't go far. It's lost itself, the nassty nosey thing. It doesn't know the way out. It said so."

"It said so, yes; but it's tricksy. It doesn't say what it means. It won't say what it's got in its pocketses. It knows. It knows a way in, it must know a way out, yes. It's off to the back-door. To the back-door, that's it."

"The goblinses will catch it then. It can't get out that way, precious."

"Ssss, sss, gollum! Goblinses! Yes, but if it's got the present, our precious present, then goblinses will get it, gollum! They'll find it, they'll find out what it does. We shan't ever be safe again, never, gollum! One of the goblinses will put it on, and then no one will see him. He'll be there but not seen. Not even our clever eyeses will notice him; and he'll come creepsy and tricksy and catch us, gollum, gollum!"

"Then let's stop talking, precious, and make haste. If the Baggins has gone that way, we must go quick and see. Go! Not far now. Make haste!"

With a spring Gollum got up and started shambling off at a great pace. Bilbo hurried after him, still cautiously, though his chief fear now was of tripping on another snag and falling with a noise. His head was in a whirl of hope and wonder. It seemed that the ring he had was a magic ring: it made you invisible! He had heard of such things, of course, in old old tales; but it was hard to believe that he really had found one, by accident. Still there it was: Gollum with his bright eyes had passed him by, only a yard to one side.

On they went, Gollum flip-flapping ahead, hissing and cursing; Bilbo behind going as softly as a hobbit can. Soon they came to places where, as Bilbo had noticed on the way down, side-passages opened, this way and that. Gollum began at once to count them.

"One left, yes. One right, yes. Two right, yes, yes. Two left, yes, yes." And so on and on.

As the count grew he slowed down, and he began to get shaky and weepy; for he was leaving the water further and further behind, and he was getting afraid. Goblins might be about, and he had lost his ring. At last he stopped by a low opening, on their left as they went up.

"Seven right, yes. Six left, yes!" he whispered. "This is it. This is the way to the back-door, yes. Here's the passage!"

He peered in, and shrank back. "But we durstn't go in, precious, no we durstn't. Goblinses down there. Lots of goblinses. We smells them. Ssss!"

"What shall we do? Curse them and crush them! We must wait here, precious, wait a bit and see."

So they came to a dead stop. Gollum had brought Bilbo to the way out after all, but Bilbo could not get in! There was Gollum sitting humped up right in the opening, and his eyes gleamed cold in his head, as he swayed it from side to side between his knees.

Bilbo crept away from the wall more quietly than a mouse; but Gollum stiffened at once, and sniffed, and his eyes went green. He hissed softly but menacingly. He could not see the hobbit, but now he was on the alert, and he had other senses that the darkness had sharpened: hearing and smell. He seemed to be crouched right down with his flat hands splayed on the floor, and his head thrust out, nose almost to the stone. Though he was only a black shadow in the gleam of his own eyes, Bilbo could see or feel that he was tense as a bowstring, gathered for a spring.

Bilbo almost stopped breathing, and went stiff himself. He was desperate. He must get away, out of this horrible darkness, while he had any strength left. He must fight. He must stab the foul thing, put its eyes out, kill it. It meant to kill him. No, not a fair fight. He was invisible now. Gollum had no sword. Gollum had not actually threatened to kill him, or tried to yet. And he was miserable, alone, lost. A sudden understanding, a pity mixed with horror, welled up in Bilbo's heart: a glimpse of endless unmarked days without light or hope of betterment, hard stone, cold fish, sneaking and whispering. All these thoughts passed in a flash of a second. He trembled. And then quite suddenly in another flash, as if lifted by a new strength and resolve, he leaped.

No great leap for a man, but a leap in the dark. Straight over Gollum's head he jumped, seven feet forward and three in the air; indeed, had he known it, he only just missed cracking his skull on the low arch of the passage.

Gollum threw himself backwards, and grabbed as the hobbit flew over him, but too late: his hands snapped on thin air, and Bilbo, falling fair on his sturdy feet, sped off down the new tunnel. He did not turn to see what Gollum was doing. There was a hissing and cursing almost at his heels at first, then it stopped. All at once there came a bloodcurdling shriek, filled with hatred and despair. Gollum was defeated. He dared go no further. He had lost: lost his prey, and lost, too, the only thing he had ever cared for, his precious. The cry brought Bilbo's heart to his mouth, but still he held on. Now faint as an echo, but menacing, the voice came behind:

"Thief, thief, thief! Baggins! We hates it, we hates it, we hates it for ever!"

Then there was a silence. But that too seemed menacing to Bilbo. "If goblins are so near that he smelt them," he thought, "then they'll have heard his shrieking and cursing. Careful now, or this way will lead you to worse things."

The passage was low and roughly made. It was not too difficult for the hobbit, except when, in spite of all care, he stubbed his poor toes again, several times, on nasty jagged stones in the floor. "A bit low for goblins, at least for the big ones," thought Bilbo, not knowing that even the big ones, the orcs of the mountains, go along at a great speed stooping low with their hands almost on the ground.

Soon the passage that had been sloping down began to go up again, and after a while it climbed steeply. That slowed Bilbo

down. But at last the slope stopped, the passage turned a corner, and dipped down again, and there, at the bottom of a short
incline, he saw, filtering round another corner—a glimpse of
light. Not red light, as of fire or lantern, but a pale out-of-doors
sort of light. Then Bilbo began to run.

Scuttling as fast as his legs would carry him he turned the
last corner and came suddenly right into an open space, where
the light, after all that time in the dark, seemed dazzlingly
bright. Really it was only a leak of sunshine in through a doorway, where a great door, a stone door, was left standing open.

Bilbo blinked, and then suddenly he saw the goblins: goblins
in full armour with drawn swords sitting just inside the door,
and watching it with wide eyes, and watching the passage that
led to it. They were aroused, alert, ready for anything.

They saw him sooner than he saw them. Yes, they saw him.
Whether it was an accident, or a last trick of the ring before it
took a new master, it was not on his finger. With yells of delight
the goblins rushed upon him.

A pang of fear and loss, like an echo of Gollum's misery,
smote Bilbo, and forgetting even to draw his sword he stuck
his hands into his pockets. And there was the ring still, in his
left pocket, and it slipped on his finger. The goblins stopped
short. They could not see a sign of him. He had vanished. They
yelled twice as loud as before, but not so delightedly.

"Where is it?" they cried.

"Go back up the passage!" some shouted.

"This way!" some yelled. "That way!" others yelled.

"Look out for the door," bellowed the captain.

Whistles blew, armour clashed, swords rattled, goblins
cursed and swore and ran hither and thither, falling over one
another and getting very angry. There was a terrible outcry, to-
do, and disturbance.

Bilbo was dreadfully frightened, but he had the sense to understand what had happened and to sneak behind a big barrel
which held drink for the goblin-guards, and so get out of the
way and avoid being bumped into, trampled to death, or caught
by feel.

"I must get to the door, I must get to the door!" he kept on
saying to himself, but it was a long time before he ventured to
try. Then it was like a horrible game of blindman's buff. The
place was full of goblins running about, and the poor little hobbit dodged this way and that, was knocked over by a goblin who
could not make out what he had bumped into, scrambled away

on all fours, slipped between the legs of the captain just in time, got up, and ran for the door.

It was still ajar, but a goblin had pushed it nearly to. Bilbo struggled but he could not move it. He tried to squeeze through the crack. He squeezed and squeezed, and he stuck! It was awful. His buttons had got wedged on the edge of the door and the door-post. He could see outside into the open air: there were a few steps running down into a narrow valley between tall mountains; the sun came out from behind a cloud and shone bright on the outside of the door—but he could not get through.

Suddenly one of the goblins inside shouted: "There is a shadow by the door. Something is outside!"

Bilbo's heart jumped into his mouth. He gave a terrific squirm. Buttons burst off in all directions. He was through, with a torn coat and waistcoat, leaping down the steps like a goat, while bewildered goblins were still picking up his nice brass buttons on the doorstep.

Of course they soon came down after him, hooting and hallooing, and hunting among the trees. But they don't like the sun: it makes their legs wobble and their heads giddy. They could not find Bilbo with the ring on, slipping in and out of the shadow of the trees, running quick and quiet, and keeping out of the sun; so soon they went back grumbling and cursing to guard the door. Bilbo had escaped.

Cuchulain has killed kings

W. B. Yeats

Cuchulain has killed kings,
Kings and sons of kings,
Dragons out of the water,
And witches out of the air,
Banachas and Bonachas and people of the woods.

Witches that steal the milk,
Fomor that steal the children,
Hags that have heads like hares,
Hares that have claws like witches,
All riding a-cock-horse
Out of the very bottom of the bitter black North.

He has killed kings,
Kings and the sons of kings,
Dragons out of the water,
And witches out of the air,
Banachas and Bonachas and people of the woods.

Death of a Maiden

Rosemary Sutcliff

Years have passed since King Arthur drew the sword from the stone, formed his fabled Round Table of knights, and became King of England. Peace and justice reign throughout the land, and yet Arthur's knights are troubled. With all the great deeds behind them, and nothing to look forward to, they grow restless and bored. Suddenly, a vision of the Holy Grail appears before Arthur and his knights, and a voice commands them to search for it. Dissolving the Round Table, they eagerly set forth. However, the Quest is a long and a difficult one— several knights give up, and many more die. Finally, only three knights—Galahad, Percival, and Bors—remain. Together with Percival's sister, Anchoret, they continue the quest.

SO the three knights and the maiden returned to their own ship; and as soon as they were on board the wind caught and filled the sail and carried them swiftly from the islet.

More days passed; and one morning the ship came sailing into a small land-locked harbor far to the north of any lands that they had known before. And since it seemed to them that their ship would not have brought them so surely to this landfall, if it were not for some purpose, they went ashore and took the track which ran up from the waterside and looked as though it must lead to some living-place of men.

Presently the track lifted over a moorland ridge, and they saw before them the dark mass of a castle rising like a rock-crag from the heather that washed to its walls. And as they stood looking, ten knights came riding out through the castle gateway; and behind them a maiden carrying a great silver bowl.

When they came up, the leader of the troop spoke to Sir Galahad, with no courtesy of greeting. "The maiden you have with you is of noble birth?"

"She is the daughter of a king and of a queen," said Sir Galahad.

"Has she ever sinned?"

"Never. That is known to all of us, by certain signs of a ship and of a sword belt."

"Then she must obey the custom of the castle."

"I am weary of the customs of castles," said Galahad. "What is this one?"

"It is that every maiden of noble birth to pass this way must pay passage dues, not in gold, but in blood from her right arm."

"That is an ugly custom," said Galahad.

And Percival moved closer to his sister.

"It is still the custom," said the leader, urging his horse closer. "The dues must be paid."

"Not while the strength is in my sword arm," said Galahad.

"Or in mine," said Percival.

"Or yet in mine," said Bors.

And as the knights came thrusting about them, they drew their swords and turned shoulder to shoulder, facing outwards all ways, with the maiden Anchoret in their midst. And when the knights charged in on them, they hurled them back. But scarcely was the fighting begun, when a score more knights came riding out from the castle and ringed them round. Then the attackers drew back a little, panting. "You are three valiant fighting-men," said the leader, "and so we have no wish to kill you. But even you cannot burst out of this circle; and as to the maiden, it will be all one in the end. Yield her up now, and go free."

"Such freedom would not taste over-sweet," said Galahad.

"Then you are bent on dying?"

"As God wills. But it is not yet come to that." Galahad brought up his sword.

Then the fighting burst out again, fierce and furious; and the knights drove in upon the three companions from all sides. All day they fought, until the shadows grew long and were lost in dusk, and the dusk deepened into the dark and they could no longer see the sword strokes. Then a trumpet sounded from the castle to break off the fray. And as the three stood leaning on their weary swords, the horsemen still ringed around them, more men came from the castle, bearing torches, and behind the torch-bearers an old white-haired man with a gold chain about his neck, who said to the companions, "Sirs, the last of the fighting-light is gone from the sky. Therefore it is time to call a truce. Do you come back now with us to the castle, and have safe lodging for the night. No harm shall come to you nor to the maiden while darkness lasts, and in the morning you shall all return to this place and state in which you stand now, and the fighting shall go forward as though there had been no pause between one sword-stroke and the next."

And the maiden Anchoret said, "Let us go with them. We shall be safe under the truce; and I know in my heart that this is the thing we are to do."

So they went with the old man and the castle knights, through the deep gateway into the stronghold. And there they were made welcome as honored guests. And when supper was over in the Great Hall, the old man told them more concerning the custom of the castle.

"Some two years ago, the lady of this place, whose knights we are, fell sick of that dread disease, leprosy. We sent for every physician far and near, but none could heal her sickness. At last, a wise man told us that if she were bathed with the blood of a maiden, who was of noble birth, and who had never sinned in fact or in thought, our mistress would be instantly healed. Therefore no high-born maiden passes this way, that we do not take from her a bowlful of her blood. That is all the story."

"And yet the blood of these maidens has not healed your lady," said Sir Bors.

"Alas, no. It must be that none to pass this way so far has been altogether without sin."

When the telling was done, the maiden Anchoret called her three companions to her, and said, "Sirs, you have heard how it is with this lady, and that it lies in my power to give her healing. Now I know for what purpose the ship has brought us to this morning's harbor."

"If you do this thing," said Galahad, "I think that you will lose your life to save hers."

"That I know," said Anchoret. "But I know also, as I have known from the moment that I was told to cut my hair, what pathway I follow. Therefore let the three of you, who are most dear to me, give me your leave, for I would sooner do this with your leave and your blessing than without."

Then the three bowed their heads and gave her the leave that she asked for.

And she called to all those in the hall, "Be happy! For tomorrow your lady shall be well again!"

Next morning, they heard Mass together, and then returned to the Great Hall. And the people of the castle brought their lady from the chamber where she lay. And as she came, horror rose in Bors and Percival, and despite themselves they gave back a little at sight of her terrible leper's face when she put back her veil. Only Sir Galahad stood his ground, and bowed to her gravely in all courtesy; and the maiden Anchoret moved forward.

147

"You are come to heal me?" said the lady, as well as she could through her crumbling lips.

"Lady, I come, and I am ready. Let them bring the bowl."

Then the same maiden who had followed the knights out from the castle yesterday came carrying the same silver bowl. And standing before them all as straight and sweet as a young poplar tree, Anchoret held out her arm over it, and the old man brought a little bright knife, and opened one of the veins that showed blue under her fair skin, like the branching veins on an iris petal.

The red blood sprang out, and swiftly the bowl began to fill.

When it was almost brimming, Anchoret began to sway on her feet, as though a cold wind were in the slender branches of the poplar tree. She turned her face to the lady, and said, "Madam, to give you healing, I am come to my death. Pray for my soul."

And with the words scarce spoken, she fell back fainting into the arms of the three companions who sprang forward to catch her.

They laid her down, and did all that might be done to staunch the bleeding, but it had gone too far with her.

She opened her eyes after a while, but they all knew that she was dying; and when she spoke to Percival, her voice had grown so faint and far away that he had to bend close to catch her words.

"Dear brother, I beg you not to leave my body buried in this country. But as soon as my life is gone, carry me back to the ship, and let me go where fate and the wind shall bear me. I promise you this, that whenever you reach the holy city of Sarras, where the Grail Quest will assuredly take you in the end, you will find me there. And in that city, and nowhere else, pray you make my grave."

Weeping, Percival promised her.

She spoke once more, "Tomorrow, part from each other and go your separate ways, until your paths shall bring you together again to the Grail Castle of Corbenic. This, through me, is Our Lord's command to you."

And she gave the quietest of sighs, and the life went out from her.

And within the hour, when she had been bathed with the blood of the maiden, the lady of the castle was whole and well again, her blackened and hideous flesh restored to all its bloom; and she was young and beautiful once more, to the great rejoicing of all her people.

But Galahad and Percival and Bors set about their own tasks in sorrow. And when she had been made ready and all things fitly done, they carried the maiden's body on a litter spread with softest silks, back to the ship waiting in the harbor, and laid her there amidships. And Percival her brother set between her folded hands a letter he had written, telling who she was and how she had come to die, and setting forth on fair parchment the events of the Grail Quest in which she had taken part, that anyone who found her body on foreign shores might treat it with the more honor, knowing all her story.

Then they pushed the vessel off from the shore, and watched her drift quietly out to sea. For as long as they could still see the ship, they waited on the water's side; and when she was quite gone, they turned back to the castle.

The lady and her knights would have had them enter and rest, but they would not set foot in the place again, but asked that their arms should be brought out to them. So the people of the castle brought out their harness and weapons, and for each of them a horse, and they armed themselves and mounted, and set forth on their way once more.

But they had not gone far when great storm clouds began to gather, and it grew dark as late evening, though it was scarce past noon. And seeing a chapel beside the track, they stabled their horses in a rough shelter outside, and went in. Hardly had they done so, when the bulging black bellies of the storm clouds burst into thunder and lightning and lashing rain. And looking back from their shelter, the way that they had come, they saw the whole sky split open above the castle, and flaming thunderbolts hurtling down upon it. And above the roar of the tempest, they could hear the crash of falling towers.

All night the storm raged, but towards dawn the thunder ceased and the clouds parted and drifted away, and the sky grew clear and gentle, washed with light from the sun that was not yet risen.

Then the three companions rode back to see what had become of the castle. When they came to the gatehouse, it was scorched and ruined; and riding inside they found nothing but fallen stones and the bodies of men and women lying where the tempest of God's wrath had struck them down.

The lady of the castle had not kept her restored health and beauty long.

"The ways of the Grail Quest are indeed strange past men's understanding," said Percival, thinking of his sister.

They dismounted and hitched their horses to some fallen roof timbers in the courtyard, and went looking from place to place to see if any living thing yet survived. And so they came at last to the castle chapel, and behind it a small enclosed burial ground, with soft green grass, and late-flowering white roses arching their thorny sprays over the gravestones, a pleasant and peaceful place, and the storm had passed it by untouched. And as they moved among the stones, reading the names on each, they knew that it was the resting place of all the other maidens who had died for the sake of the lady.

After a while, they turned away and went back to their horses, and rode together until the moor was passed and the dark trees of the forest came to meet them. And there they checked, and took their leave of each other, as the maiden Anchoret had bidden them. "God keep you," they said, "God bring us all to our meeting place again at Corbenic Castle."

And they rode their three separate ways into the forest. . . .

Jacob Parrott: The First Medal of Honor Recipient

from Congressional Medal of Honor Recipients

Kieran Doherty

IN early April of 1862, a young Union Army soldier was called from his tent in a camp in Tennessee. "My captain," he said later, ". . . asked me if I would go on a secret expedition, and told me that, if I agreed to go, I should go up to his tent . . . and report to him. I went up and told him I would go."

In this way, Jacob Parrott, an eighteen-year-old private from Ohio, was chosen for what came to be known as the Andrews Raid. For his part in this raid, Parrott became the first man to receive the Medal of Honor.

At the time of the raid, the Civil War had been going on for almost one year. As the Battle of Shiloh raged in western Tennessee, two men met in the eastern part of that state, far from the fighting. One of the men, Brigadier General Ormsby Mitchel, was in command of the Union Army unit in the area. The other, James Andrews, was a Virginia native and a Union spy. That night, Andrews put forth a daring plan. He would lead two dozen men on a raid far behind the Rebel lines. They would burn bridges and tear up track on the train line between Atlanta, Georgia, and Chattanooga, Tennessee. In those days, rail lines carried almost all freight and passengers between major cities. With trains unable to reach Chattanooga from Atlanta, the Tennessee city would be cut off. It would fall to Mitchel's troops. The general wanted to capture Chattanooga. He gave his approval.

The next day, Andrews began recruiting men for his raid. Jacob Parrott was one of the first to volunteer.

Little is known of Parrott's life before he joined the army. We do know he was from Hardin County, Ohio. We know his parents were dead when he enlisted and that he was a farmer before joining the army.

On the night of Monday, April 7, Parrott and twenty-three other men met with Andrews outside Shelbyville, Tennessee. It was a wild night. The wind moaned in the trees. Lightning flashed, and thunder rumbled like the sound of far-off cannon.

As the men stood on a rise near a rail track, Andrews laid out his plan. He told the raiders to travel in small groups to Marietta, Georgia, about thirty miles north of Atlanta. Dressed in civilian clothes and carrying pistols, they were to board a northbound train. He would already be on the train. At a signal from him, they would capture the train and race north with it. They would burn bridges and tear up track as they went. Andrews warned the men that if they were caught they would face death as spies. He gave them a chance to back out of the planned raid. "No one, however, showed the faintest desire to avail himself of this offer," recalled Corporal William Pittinger, one of the raiders. That very night, the raiders headed south. In addition to Parrott and Andrews, the raiding party included three sergeants, Pittinger and four other corporals, fourteen privates, and one civilian, William Campbell. The soldiers were all from Ohio regiments.

Parrott and nineteen-year-old Private Samuel Robertson set out together. That night they stumbled ten miles in the darkness. They waded through knee-deep mud, soaked by a heavy rain. Finally, they took refuge in a shed. In the morning, they rose and began walking again. For four days and nights, the two young men trudged through the rain across enemy territory.

In the predawn hours of April 12, Parrott and eighteen other raiders entered the Marietta train station. (Five of the men were missing. Three never made it to the depot, and two came late.) Andrews, as planned, had gone on to Atlanta. While his men were gathering in Marietta, he boarded a northbound train. At about 5 A.M., Parrott and the others bought one-way tickets to the town of Big Shanty, eight miles north. In minutes, the train from Atlanta, with Andrews on board, pulled into the station. At 5:15 A.M., with the raiders on board, it headed north, pulled by a powerful engine known as the *General*. Soon, it came to a stop in Big Shanty. The conductor called out, "Twenty minutes for breakfast." When the passengers, conductor, and engineer climbed off to eat breakfast at a hotel near the station, Andrews gave his signal, and his men struck.

Quickly the raiders uncoupled the engine and three boxcars from the rest of the train. Andrews, with two men who knew how to operate an engine, got into the *General's* cab. The others climbed into the boxcars. At a nod from Andrews, the engine and cars lurched into motion. The raiders had done it! They'd stolen a rebel train!

As the raiders steamed north, they stopped the train several times. They tore up tracks and cut telegraph lines. In this way, they thought, they would delay any pursuers. They were wrong.

The *General's* engineer, Jeff Cain, conductor William Fuller, and a mechanic, Anthony Murphy, heard the train pull away from Big Shanty. They sprinted from the hotel by the tracks and ran after the train on foot. A few miles up the track, the three men found a handcart. They jumped on the cart and continued the chase. Soon they found an engine, the *Yonah,* parked on a siding, ready to roll. They leaped onto the *Yonah* and steamed after the raiders. After just a few miles, they had to abandon the *Yonah* when they came to a spot where southbound freight trains blocked their way. Soon, though, they found another engine, the *William R. Smith.* They chased after the raiders in the *Smith* until they were forced to abandon that engine as well. Still, luck was with the Southern railroad men. After running several miles up the track, they found yet another engine. It was the *Texas.*

The raiders, meanwhile, had stopped several times to wait on sidings for southbound trains to pass and then to tear up track. One of the men later said they were working on the rails when, "not far behind us we heard the scream of a locomotive bearing down on us at lightning speed." It was the *Texas,* with Fuller, Murphy, and Cain on board.

The raiders jumped back on the stolen train. They raced north, toward the Union Army lines. But now the rebels were close behind. Andrews and his men threw rail ties on the tracks, trying to slow the *Texas.* Nothing worked. Finally, just five miles from the Tennessee border, the *General* ran out of fuel. Andrews told the raiders it was every man for himself. They should abandon the train and try to make their way back to the Union lines. They jumped from the train and fled into the surrounding woods.

Within a week, all the raiders who had made it to Marietta were captured, including the two who missed the train. Soon after his capture, Parrott was flogged by a Confederate officer. "I suppose, as I was the youngest, they thought they could make me [talk]; but I wouldn't tell them anything," he later said.

Soon after their capture, Andrews and seven of his men were hanged as spies. One of those hanged was Private Robertson.

For a time, it looked as if all the men would be put to death. However, the rebels feared that some of their men in Union hands would be hanged if any more of the raiders were killed. They let Parrott and the other men live. In October, Parrott and the others escaped. Eight made their way to freedom, but six, including Parrott, were recaptured.

For the next five months, Parrott and the others remained in prison. Finally, in March of 1863, they were set free.

Later that month, the six freed men met with Secretary of War Edwin Stanton in Washington. With Parrott at that meeting were Pittinger, Privates William Bensinger and Robert Buffum, Sergeant Elihu Mason, and Corporal William Reddick.

Pittinger later said that Stanton "seemed especially pleased" with Parrott. The secretary offered Parrott a chance to attend West Point Military Academy. Pittinger recalled that Parrott said that he "would rather go back and fight the rebels who had used him so badly."

Stanton also told the six men they would be "great heroes" when they returned to their homes. He then left the room and came back holding a medal. Congress, he said, had ordered new medals to be prepared to honor soldiers and sailors for valor. "[Y]our party shall have the first," he said. He then handed the medal to Jacob Parrott, the first man ever to be presented with the Medal of Honor.

Soon after the meeting with Stanton, Parrott went back to war. He fought in the Battle of Atlanta. Later, he took part in a great victory march in the nation's capital. After the war, he went back to Ohio, where he became a successful businessman. He died in 1912.

Eventually, almost all the raiders were given Medals of Honor. Andrews and Campbell did not get medals because they were civilians. A third raider was not honored when it was discovered that he had enlisted and served under an assumed name. Of all those men who received medals, though, Jacob Parrott has a special place in history as the first man to be awarded his nation's highest military honor.

There Is No Sanctuary for Brave Men

A. G. Herbertson

There is no sanctuary for brave men,
   Danger allures them as it were a sun;
What they have dared they will dare once again
   And so continue till the day is done.

There is no satiation of brave deeds,
   One draws another as wit calls on wit,
Oh, what a soul it is that ever heeds
   The hour's necessity and springs to it!

There's no intimidation of great thought,
   Knowledge attracts it as the heavens the eye;
Though dangerous 'tis to learn, it will be taught,
   Pushing its question to the uttermost Why.

There is no sanctuary for brave men,
   Danger allures them as the moon the tide;
What they have dared they will dare once again
   Though they lose all else in the world beside.

from

Raiders of the Lost Ark

Les Martin

THE year was 1936. In Germany, Adolf Hitler had risen to supreme power as head of the Nazi Party, and was arming his country for war.

In Washington, D.C., the leaders of the United States watched uneasily as the shadow of Nazi imperialism fell over Europe.

But even as the threat of global war grew every day, most Americans were thinking of their own personal difficulties, their own hopes and dreams.

This was certainly true of Indiana Jones. Indy stood in a clearing deep in a South American jungle. His handsome face was streaked with grime and sweat under his battered felt hat. His chin was covered with stubble. For days he and his two Peruvian guides had been struggling through the uncharted green maze of the tropical rain forest. But now, as he looked across the clearing he had come to, Indy forgot how tired he had been. He felt fresh and strong and eager.

At last, Indy had found the entrance to the ancient temple he had been searching for. Long ago, Chachapoyan Indians had built this temple to protect a small golden statue they worshipped as a god. Somewhere inside the temple was the statue.

Indiana Jones wanted that statue. He wanted it very badly. Nothing was going to stop him from getting it. Not all the cunning defenses of the ancient temple builders. And not the modern pistol that was pointing at him right now.

Barranca, one of Indy's guides, held the pistol. Barranca had decided that he wanted the golden statue for himself.

Indy's hand moved to the back of his leather jacket faster than Barranca could blink. Out from under the jacket came a tightly curled bullwhip. The ten-foot leather lash of the whip whistled through the air. It wrapped around Barranca's gun hand, jerking the guide's hand down. The gun went off, and the bullet buried itself in the ground. With a gasp of pain, Barranca let the pistol drop.

"You'd better leave it there," advised Indy. "I'd rather not have to show you what else this whip can do."

Barranca looked at the whip resting lightly in Indy's hand. Without a word, he turned and fled into the jungle.

"That Barranca was crazy," said Satipo, the second guide. "But you can trust me, *Señor.* I am your loyal servant. You can put away your whip."

"We'll see how loyal you are," said Indy. "Follow me. We're going into the temple."

"But the curse," Satipo protested fearfully. "It is my duty as your guide to warn you of the Curse of the Ancients."

"Come *on,* Satipo," Indy said. "A little thing like the threat of death shouldn't discourage you. It's all part of the job."

Indy led the way inside. Holding lighted torches, the two men scrambled down a stone incline and along a twisting tunnel. Tarantulas scurried underfoot. The air was heavy with the smell of centuries. Then, around a turn in the tunnel, the two men saw the end of the passageway, ablaze with light.

The sight made Satipo forget his fear. He pressed forward past Indy—and screamed.

The guide had stepped into empty space. He was falling into a bottomless hole concealed by a layer of cobwebs. Just in time, Indy grabbed Satipo's belt and pulled him back.

"We must stop now," said Satipo, shaking with fear. "There is no way we can go around this hole."

Indy looked upward. "But we can go *over* it," he said.

Satipo was puzzled. "How, *Señor?*"

"With this." Indy drew out his whip and lashed the end of it around a root hanging from the ceiling. "Do you want to be first across, Satipo?"

The terrified look on Satipo's face was answer enough. Indy took hold of the whip handle and swung himself easily across the yawning black pit. Then he swung the whip back to Satipo. Satipo's mouth moved in a silent prayer. Holding on to the whip for dear life, the guide landed next to Indy with a thud.

"Nothing like a little fun to liven up a trip," said Indy. "Now let's see about getting the idol."

A moment later they were at the end of the passageway, staring into a small stone chamber. Its floor was made of tile, laid in an intricate design. Its walls were decorated with a strange pattern of thousands of tiny holes. In the middle of the room, sitting on a stone altar, was the golden idol. Indy's breath stopped when he saw it. Lit by a single shaft of bright sunlight, the gleaming statue looked both beautiful and eerie.

"So, there is nothing to fear after all," said Satipo. "We have not been hurt. Let me get the idol for you." He started into the chamber.

"No!" Indy blocked Satipo's way. Without another word, he picked up a stick and tapped one of the border tiles. Nothing happened. Then he tapped a center tile. Suddenly there was a rush of air and a whistling sound. A swarm of deadly darts flew from the tiny holes in the wall. They were aimed to kill any intruder.

"I thought our ancient friends would try to defend their god," said Indy. "I'm glad they didn't disappoint me."

Careful to step only on the border tiles, Indy made his way across the room to where the idol rested. He stood enjoying his first good look at it. To some people, the gold statue might have looked ugly, even frightening. To Indy, it was a feast of beauty. Looking at it made him feel as if he had stepped back through time. He reached out to grasp the statue and then remembered where he was.

Indy drew his hand back. He could sense the genius of the temple builders all around him. What other cunning traps had they laid to protect their precious idol? He was sure he hadn't outwitted them yet.

Indy emptied out his leather coin pouch. Then he filled it with dirt from around the altar base. He weighed the pouch in his palm. It might—just might—now weigh the same as the idol. If he put the pouch in the idol's place at the exact moment that he lifted the idol from the altar, chances were he might—just might—get away with the switch.

"There's only one way to find out," Indy said to himself. He made the switch. For a moment, nothing happened. Then a stone slab on the altar fell with a sharp click. Indy heard a deep rumbling from behind the chamber walls. It grew louder, and the entire temple started to shake.

Clutching the idol, Indy raced back on the border tiles to the doorway. Satipo had already started down the passageway ahead of him, and was using the whip to swing across the pit.

When he was safely on the other side, Satipo shouted, "Throw me the idol. Then I will give you back your whip."

A falling stone from the ceiling hit Indy's cheek. He had no time to argue. He tossed the idol to Satipo. Satipo caught the idol and stuffed it into his jacket. Then he dropped the whip on the ground. *"Adios, amigo,"* he shouted to Indy, and disappeared around the curve in the tunnel.

Indy didn't bother to answer. With every ounce of his strength, he hurled himself across the pit. He fell short, and began a sickening drop down. Then his clawing fingers caught the side of the pit. Painfully, he pulled himself up.

Above the rumbling of the collapsing temple came an anguished scream. It was Satipo. When Indy reached him, the thief was dead. Long spikes had sprung out of the wall and into his fleeing body. The curse had claimed its victim.

"*Adios, amigo,*" said Indy as he took the idol from Satipo's jacket. He had no time to lose. The walls of the passageway were crumbling. The stone floor was splitting apart. With his lungs bursting, Indy made it out of the temple seconds before it caved in.

Panting, he threw himself on the ground. He looked at the idol glowing in the sunshine. He grinned. Nearby, on a jungle river, a seaplane waited to fly him back to civilization. Soon the idol would rest in a museum, where the world could enjoy its beauty. At a moment like this, Indy knew why he loved taking risks. Beating all the odds made triumph taste delicious.

Suddenly, Indy's grin faded. On the ground he saw a shadow lengthening toward the idol. He looked up to meet the amused glance of his greatest rival—the Frenchman René Belloq.

Belloq, like Indy, was an archaeologist who loved to hunt the lost treasures of the past. Like Indy he possessed great knowledge and great determination. But there the resemblances ended. Indy's discoveries went to universities and museums, where they could be studied and enjoyed. Belloq's were hoarded for his solitary pleasure—or sold to private collectors for huge sums of money. The Frenchman was dishonest, clever, and ruthless. Indy despised him.

Even deep in the jungle, Belloq looked elegant. His safari suit was spotless. His pith helmet was white. His boots were as brightly polished as his smile.

"We meet again," said Belloq. "As always, it is a pleasure to see you, Indy Jones. You've gone to such trouble to get me something I want. Now, please, give me the idol. Unless you prefer to argue with my friends."

Belloq was flanked by two giant Hovitos warriors. Their glistening bodies were bright with war paint, their blowguns ready to spit out poison darts. At the jungle's edge were thirty more warriors.

"When you put it so politely, how can I say no?" said Indy with a wry grimace. He got to his feet, holding out the idol to Belloq. Belloq grabbed it eagerly, and made the mistake Indy had been hoping for.

Belloq held the idol high above his head for the Hovitos warriors to admire. Instantly they fell to their knees before the god of their ancestors. Belloq just can't resist playing god, Indy thought. Then he made his break into the jungle.

In a flash, Belloq and the Hovitos were after him. Indy could hear them gaining on him as he fought his way through the thick foliage. He barely made it to the edge of a high cliff. Far below was the river, where his seaplane waited. There was just one way to reach it. Indy dove. He swam to the plane and dragged himself aboard, drenched and gasping for breath. "Get it going," he said to the pilot, "or we're both dead men."

As the plane lifted into the sky, Indy looked down at the jungle. But all he could see in his mind was the idol in Belloq's hand. "Enjoy it while you can, Belloq," Indy muttered. "When I catch up with you, I'm going to make you pay for it and everything else you've stolen—with interest."

The Reluctant Jedi

from Star Wars

George Lucas

The Jedi Knights, protectors of the Old Republic, were gone—destroyed by one of their own, the treacherous Darth Vader. With the passing of the Jedi, the Old Republic soon fell, only to be replaced by the heartless Imperial Empire. A resistance movement is organized to combat the cruelties of the Empire. Yet the Resistance is soon imperiled by the construction of the Empire's new super weapon, the Death Star—a spaceship the size of a moon with enough fire power to shatter a planet to bits. Knowing the Death Star means their doom, the Resistance steals the plans to the Death Star and plans to contact the last Jedi they know to exist, Obi-wan Kenobi.

Both the plans and the mission to contact Kenobi are given to the Princess Leia Organa. But her ship is captured by Darth Vader, and she must trust the Death Star plans, as well as the mission to contact Kenobi, to her android Artoo Detoo. Escaping the doomed ship, Artoo flees to the planet Tatooine with his 'droid companion See Threepio. They are soon captured by the natives of the planet, and sold to Luke Skywalker's uncle.

But Artoo remains determined to fulfill his mission, and escapes. Luke tracks down the 'droid, and comes face to face with Obi-wan Kenobi—better known to him as Old Ben.

WHILE Luke was thus occupied, Kenobi's attention was concentrated on Artoo Detoo. The squat 'droid sat passively on the cool cavern floor while the old man fiddled with its metal insides. Finally the man sat back with a "Humph!" of satisfaction and closed the open panels in the robot's rounded head. "Now let's see if we can figure out what you are, my little friend, and where you came from."

Luke was almost finished anyway, and Kenobi's words were sufficient to pull him away from the repair area. "I saw part of the message," he began, "and I . . ."

Once more the striking portrait was being projected into

empty space from the front of the little robot. Luke broke off, enraptured by its enigmatic beauty once again.

"Yes, I think that's got it," Kenobi murmured contemplatively.

The image continued to flicker, indicating a tape hastily prepared. But it was much sharper, better defined now, Luke noted with admiration. One thing was apparent: Kenobi was skilled in subjects more specific than desert scavenging.

"General Obi-wan Kenobi," the mellifluous voice was saying, "I present myself in the name of the world family of Alderaan and of the Alliance to Restore the Republic. I break your solitude at the bidding of my father, Bail Organa, Viceroy and First Chairman of the Alderaan system."

Kenobi absorbed this extraordinary declamation while Luke's eyes bugged big enough to fall from his face.

"Years ago, General," the voice continued, "you served the Old Republic in the Clone Wars. Now my father begs you to aid us again in our most desperate hour. We would have you join him on Alderaan. You *must* go to him.

"I regret that I am unable to present my father's request to you in person. My mission to meet personally with you has failed. Hence I have been forced to resort to this secondary method of communication.

"Information vital to the survival of the Alliance has been secured in the mind of this Detoo 'droid. My father will know how to retrieve it. I plead with you to see this unit safely delivered to Alderaan."

She paused, and when she continued, her words were hurried and less laced with formality. "You *must* help me, Obi-wan Kenobi. You are my last hope. I will be captured by agents of the Empire. They will learn nothing from me. Everything to be learned lies locked in the memory cells of this 'droid. Do not fail us, Obi-wan Kenobi. Do not fail *me*."

A small cloud of tridimensional static replaced the delicate portrait, then it vanished entirely. Artoo Detoo gazed up expectantly at Kenobi.

Luke's mind was as muddy as a pond laced with petroleum. Unanchored, his thoughts and eyes turned for stability to the quiet figure seated nearby.

The old man. The crazy wizard. The desert bum and all-around character whom his uncle and everyone else had known of for as long as Luke could recall.

If the breathless, anxiety-ridden message the unknown woman had just spoken into the cool air of the cave had affected

Kenobi in any way he gave no hint of it. Instead, he leaned back against the rock wall and tugged thoughtfully at his beard, puffing slowly on a water pipe of free-form tarnished chrome.

Luke visualized that simple yet lovely portrait. "She's so—so—" His farming background didn't provide him with the requisite words. Suddenly something in the message caused him to stare disbelievingly at the oldster. "General Kenobi, you fought in the Clone Wars? But . . . that was so long ago."

"Um, yes," Kenobi acknowledged, as casually as he might have discussed the recipe for shang stew. "I guess it was a while back. I was a Jedi knight once. Like," he added, watching the youth appraisingly, "your father."

"A Jedi knight," Luke echoed. Then he looked confused. "But my father didn't fight in the Clone Wars. He was no knight—just a navigator on a space freighter."

Kenobi's smile enfolded the pipe's mouthpiece. "Or so your uncle has told you." His attention was suddenly focused elsewhere. "Owen Lars didn't agree with your father's ideas, opinions, or with his philosophy of life. He believed that your father should have stayed here on Tatooine and not gotten involved in . . ." Again the seemingly indifferent shrug. "Well, he thought he should have remained here and minded his farming."

Luke said nothing, his body tense as the old man related bits and pieces of a personal history Luke had viewed only through his uncle's distortions.

"Owen was always afraid that your father's adventurous life might influence you, might pull you away from Anchorhead." He shook his head slowly, regretfully at the remembrance. "I'm afraid there wasn't much of the farmer in your father."

Luke turned away. He returned to cleaning the last particles of sand from Threepio's healing armature. "I wish I'd known him," he finally whispered.

"He was the best pilot I ever knew," Kenobi went on, "and a smart fighter. The force . . . the instinct was strong in him." For a brief second Kenobi actually appeared old. "He was also a good friend."

Suddenly the boyish twinkle returned to those piercing eyes along with the old man's natural humor. "I understand you're quite a pilot yourself. Piloting and navigation aren't hereditary, but a number of the things that can combine to make a good small-ship pilot are. Those you may have inherited. Still, even a duck has to be taught to swim."

"What's a duck?" Luke asked curiously.

"Never mind. In many ways, you know, you are much like your father." Kenobi's unabashed look of evaluation made Luke nervous. "You've grown up quite a bit since the last time I saw you."

Having no reply for that, Luke waited silently as Kenobi sank back into deep contemplation. After a while the old man stirred, evidently having reached an important decision.

"All this reminds me," he declared with deceptive casualness, "I have something here for you." He rose and walked over to a bulky, old-fashioned chest and started rummaging through it. All sorts of intriguing items were removed and shoved around, only to be placed back in the bin. A few of them Luke recognized. As Kenobi was obviously intent on something important, he forbore inquiring about any of the other tantalizing flotsam.

"When you were old enough," Kenobi was saying, "your father wanted you to have this . . . if I can ever find the blasted device. I tried to give it to you once before, but your uncle wouldn't allow it. He believed you might get some crazy ideas from it and end up following old Obi-wan on some idealistic crusade.

"You see, Luke, that's where your father and your uncle Owen disagreed. Lars is not a man to let idealism interfere with business, whereas your father didn't think the question even worth discussing. His decision on such matters came like his piloting—instinctively."

Luke nodded. He finished picking out the last of the grit and looked around for one remaining component to snap back into Threepio's open chest plate. Locating the restraining module, he opened the receiving latches in the machine and set about locking it back in place. Threepio watched the process and appeared to wince ever so perceptibly.

Luke stared into those metal and plastic photoreceptors for a long moment. Then he set the module pointedly on the workbench and closed the 'droid up. Threepio said nothing.

A grunt came from behind them, and Luke turned to see a pleased Kenobi walking over. He handed Luke a small, innocuous-looking device, which the youth studied with interest.

It consisted primarily of a short, thick handgrip with a couple of small switches set into the grip. Above this small post was a circular metal disk barely larger in diameter than his spread palm. A number of unfamiliar, jewellike components were built into both handle and disk, including what looked like the smallest power cell Luke had ever seen. The reverse side of the disk was polished to a mirror brightness. But it was the power cell that puzzled Luke the most. Whatever the thing was, it required a great deal of energy, according to the rating form of the cell.

Despite the claim that it had belonged to his father, the gizmo looked newly manufactured. Kenobi had obviously kept it carefully. Only a number of minute scratches on the handgrip hinted at previous usage.

"Sir?" came a familiar voice Luke hadn't heard in a while.

"What?" Luke was startled out of his examination.

"If you'll not be needing me," Threepio declared, "I think I'll shut down for a bit. It will help the armature nerves to knit, and I'm due for some internal self-cleansing anyhow."

"Sure, go ahead," Luke said absently, returning to his fascinated study of the whatever-it-was. Behind him, Threepio became silent, the glow fading temporarily from his eyes. Luke noticed that Kenobi was watching him with interest. "What is it?" he finally asked, unable despite his best efforts to identify the device.

"Your father's lightsaber," Kenobi told him. "At one time they were widely used. Still are, in certain galactic quarters."

Luke examined the controls on the handle, then tentatively touched a brightly colored button up near the mirrored pommel. Instantly the disk put forth a blue-white beam as thick around as his thumb. It was dense to the point of opacity and a little over a meter in length. It did not fade, but remained as brilliant and intense at its far end as it did next to the disk. Strangely, Luke felt no heat from it, though he was very careful not to touch it. He knew what a lightsaber could do, though he had never seen one before. It could drill a hole right through the rock wall of Kenobi's cave—or through a human being.

"This was the formal weapon of a Jedi knight," explained Kenobi. "Not as clumsy or random as a blaster. More skill than simple sight was required for its use. An elegant weapon. It was a symbol as well. Anyone can use a blaster or fusioncutter—but to use a lightsaber *well* was a mark of someone a cut above the ordinary." He was pacing the floor of the cave as he spoke.

"For over a thousand generations, Luke, the Jedi knights were the most powerful, most respected force in the galaxy. They served as the guardians and guarantors of peace and justice in the Old Republic."

When Luke failed to ask what had happened to them since, Kenobi looked up to see that the youth was staring vacantly into space, having absorbed little if any of the oldster's instruction. Some men would have chided Luke for not paying attention. Not

Kenobi. More sensitive than most, he waited patiently until the silence weighed strong enough on Luke for him to resume speaking.

"How," he asked slowly, "did my father die?"

Kenobi hesitated, and Luke sensed that the old man had no wish to talk about this particular matter. Unlike Owen Lars, however, Kenobi was unable to take refuge in a comfortable lie.

"He was betrayed and murdered," Kenobi declared solemnly, "by a very young Jedi named Darth Vader." He was not looking at Luke. "A boy I was training. One of my brightest disciples . . . one of my greatest failures."

Kenobi resumed his pacing. "Vader used the training I gave him and the force within him for evil, to help the later corrupt Emperors. With the Jedi knights disbanded, disorganized, or dead, there were few to oppose Vader. Today they are all but extinct."

An indecipherable expression crossed Kenobi's face. "In many ways they were too good, too trusting for their own health. They put too much trust in the stability of the Republic, failing to realize that while the body might be sound, the head was growing diseased and feeble, leaving it open to manipulation by such as the Emperor.

"I wish I knew what Vader was after. Sometimes I have the feeling he is marking time in preparation for some incomprehensible abomination. Such is the destiny of one who masters the force and is consumed by its dark side."

Luke's face twisted in confusion. "A force? That's the second time you've mentioned a 'force.'"

Kenobi nodded. "I forget sometimes in whose presence I babble. Let us say simply that the force is something a Jedi must deal with. While it has never been properly explained, scientists have theorized it is an energy field generated by living things. Early man suspected its existence, yet remained in ignorance of its potential for millennia.

"Only certain individuals could recognize the force for what it was. They were mercilessly labeled: charlatans, fakers, mystics—and worse. Even fewer could make use of it. As it was usually beyond their primitive controls, it frequently was too powerful for them. They were misunderstood by their fellows—and worse."

Kenobi made a wide, all-encompassing gesture with both arms. "The force surrounds each and every one of us. Some men believe it directs our actions, and not the other way around. Knowledge of the force and how to manipulate it was what gave the Jedi his special power."

The arms came down and Kenobi stared at Luke until the youth began to fidget uncomfortably. When he spoke again it was in a tone so crisp and unaged that Luke jumped in spite of himself. "You must learn the ways of the force also, Luke—if you are to come with me to Alderaan."

"Alderaan!" Luke hopped off the repair seat, looking dazed. "I'm not going to Alderaan. I don't even know where Alderaan is." Vaporators, 'droids, harvest—abruptly the surroundings seemed to close in on him, the formerly intriguing furnishings and alien artifacts now just a mite frightening. He looked around wildly, trying to avoid the piercing gaze of Ben Kenobi . . . old Ben . . . crazy Ben . . . General Obi-wan . . .

"I've got to get back home," he found himself muttering thickly. "It's late. I'm in for it as it is." Remembering something, he gestured toward the motionless bulk of Artoo Detoo. "You can keep the 'droid. He seems to want you to. I'll think of something to tell my uncle—I hope," he added forlornly.

"I need your help, Luke," Kenobi explained, his manner a combination of sadness and steel. "I'm getting too old for this kind of thing. Can't trust myself to finish it properly on my own. This mission is far too important." He nodded toward Artoo Detoo. "You heard and saw the message."

"But . . . I can't get involved with anything like that," protested Luke. "I've got work to do; we've got crops to bring in—even though Uncle Owen could always break down and hire a little extra help. I mean, one, I guess. But there's nothing I can do about it. Not now. Besides, that's all such a long way from here. The whole thing is really none of my business."

"That sounds like your uncle talking," Kenobi observed without rancor.

"Oh! My uncle Owen . . . How am I going to explain all this to him?"

The old man suppressed a smile, aware that Luke's destiny had already been determined for him. It had been ordained five minutes before he had learned about the manner of his father's death. It had been ordered before that when he had heard the complete message. It had been fixed in the nature of things when he had first viewed the pleading portrait of the beautiful Senator Organa awkwardly projected by the little 'droid. Kenobi shrugged inwardly. Likely it had been finalized even before the boy was born. Not that Ben believed in predestination, but he did believe in heredity—and in the force.

"Remember, Luke, the suffering of one man is the suffering of all. Distances are irrelevant to injustice. If not stopped soon enough, evil eventually reaches out to engulf all men, whether they have opposed it or ignored it."

"I suppose," Luke confessed nervously, "I *could* take you as far as Anchorhead. You can get transport from there to Mos Eisley, or wherever it is you want to go."

"Very well," agreed Kenobi. "That will do for a beginning. Then you must do what you feel is *right*."

Roads Go Ever Ever On
from The Hobbit

J.R.R. Tolkien

Roads go ever ever on,
   Over rock and under tree,
By caves where never sun has shone,
   By streams that never find the sea;
Over snow by winter sown,
   And through the merry flowers of June,
Over grass and over stone,
   And under mountains in the moon.

   Under cloud and under star,
Yet feet that wandering have gone
   Turn at last to home afar.
Eyes that fire and sword have seen
   And horror in the halls of stone
Look at last on meadows green
   And trees and hills they long have known.

Acknowledgments *(continued from p. ii)*

Estate of W. R. McAlpine

"The Young Urashima" from *Japanese Tales and Legends*, retold by Helen and William McAlpine. © Oxford University Press 1958. Reprinted by permission of Lily Gillespie and Mrs. Mary Johnson, personal representatives of the Estate of W. R. McAlpine.

Pantheon Books, a division of Random House, Inc.

"The Warrior Maiden" from *American Indian Myths and Legends* by Richard Erdoes and Alfonso Ortiz. Copyright © 1984 by Richard Erdoes and Alfonso Ortiz. Reprinted by permission of Pantheon Books, a division of Random House, Inc.

Scholastic Inc.

The Adventures of Ulysses by Bernard Evslin. Copyright © 1969 by Scholastic Inc. Reproduced by permission of Scholastic, Inc.

Simon & Schuster

"Cuchulain has killed kings" is reprinted with the permission of Simon & Schuster from *The Poems of W. B. Yeats: A New Edition*, edited by Richard J. Finneran. Copyright © 1983 by Anne Yeats.

Note: Every effort has been made to locate the copyright owner of material reprinted in this book. Omissions brought to our attention will be corrected in subsequent editions.